Iva Pezuashvili

Garbage Chute

Translated by Tamar (Tamuna) Japaridze

The book is published with the support
of the Writers' House of Georgia.

Published by BookLand Press Inc.
15 Allstate Parkway
Suite 600
Markham, Ontario L3R 5B4
Canada
www.booklandpress.com

Printed in Canada

Library and Archives Canada Cataloguing in Publication

Title: Garbage chute / Iva Pezuashvili; translated by Tamar (Tamuna) Japaridze.
Other titles: Bunkeri. English
Names: Pezuashvili, Iva, author.
Description: Translation of: Bunkeri.
Identifiers: Canadiana 2023050972X | ISBN 9781772312348 (softcover)
Classification: LCC PK9169.P49 B8613 2023 | DDC 899/.9693—dc23

Garbage Chute

Zhukovka is a small town in Russia. At present it can hardly be found on maps by anyone, be it a cartography nerd, someone with a master's degree in Geography, or even a high level 'professional Russian'. But at one time — before Gorbachev had fallen into the insanity of *Perestroika*, condemning the Soviet people to suffer from freedom diarrhea — this very Zhukovka was the well-known manufacturer of famous bicycles, which were the dream vehicles of every Young Pioneer and stripling. Those bicycles of a new generation, *Десна-два*[1], had small but durable wheels, a foldable frame, and an overly high price inflated still further by the damned black marketeers. Nevertheless, the owners of *Десна-два*, or rather their parents, were not stingy, since in the Soviet Union nothing worked so well as the institution of arousing envy. Poor Soviet parents went out of their way not to seem inferior to others and bought this 'posh' vehicle for their children. They even tried to teach them how to ride it in open daylight, in front of their neighbors, to make the relatively needy among them green with envy. Nothing was considered as kitschy as the smiling face of a child riding *Десна-два*, and since the Soviet Union itself was one solid and

---

[1] Десна-два (Russ.) – Desna-two

evil kitsch, a similar smile was often found on mosaics, posters and even postage stamps. But Soviet youngsters didn't care a monkey's fart about it; on the contrary, you should have seen how they prayed for the engineers and designers of the bicycle, praising their hands and perspicacious minds, for attaching a back seat to it. The owners of those bicycles would ride near schools, squeeze the schoolgirls into back seats, and the girls, in return, would cling passionately to their knights. Oh yes, there was something chivalrous in that act, even a bit sticky and viscous, since the Pioneer girls, to the delight of perverts, wore micro-miniskirts. They also wore snow-white socks that got greasy while riding, as the chain of *Десна-два* was always generously lubricated. So, a parent of the Soviet schoolgirl, or rather her father, noticing those greasy spots on the snow-white socks, would immediately guess that his daughter had been riding a bicycle with some 'stinker' and punished her severely. It should also be noted here that though such cases were not uncommon, we will focus on only one of them and say that the girl's name was Milla, and the name of her knight was Genna. When our brave knight Genna discovered the bruises left by a military uniform belt with a five-pointed star on his ladylove's back and buttocks, he drank a bottle of Armenian brandy, paid a visit to Milla's father Artyom—a shortie with a large ego and a fucking lieutenant sloshed after emptying two bottles of the same strong drink—and broke his ribs with a rusty cast-iron bar. So, it was in this ungentlemanly manner that he made a proposal of marriage to his greasy sweetheart.

Artyom thought about Genna's 'proposal' for quite a long time, and while he was thinking, Genna was hiding. The more Artyom thought, the more he drank, and the more he drank, the more often he waved his Makarov pistol, and more often a random bullet flew out of it. Consequently, the more often a random bullet flew out of his pistol, the more often he received a reprimand in the service. In the end, it came to the point that he was deprived of his weapon, rank and dignity at the same time. So, Genna was able to return to Yerevan safely after two years of forced exile in the city of Tbilisi, and once again made a proposal of marriage to Milla. This time he visited her family with an Italian gold wedding ring instead of the cast-iron bar.

♦　　♦　　♦

He loved his Milla with an overwhelming love and even greater passion; he loved her every night and several times a day; he loved her so incredibly and in such incredible places which were wholly inappropriate for that purpose not only for the Soviet citizens but any respectable person with a passport; he loved her at the foot of the monument of the Great Leader, in passenger cars of the brand *ноль-шесть*[2], in elevators and even in police stations, where they often found themselves stuck because of their frenzied passion; he loved her on returning home, within the walls of his parents' two-room apartment, where he showed his feelings with such violent and loud force which completely drowned out the sounds of moans and puffs, as well as the creaking of the not very high-quality springs of the Soviet bed. And now, after almost thirty years of married life, Genna missed not the extinguished fire of his once mad passion but his *Десна-два*, that permanently greasy bicycle with small wheels and a folding frame, which he dismantled before fleeing Yerevan, placing it carefully into the trunk, and bringing it proudly to Tbilisi — the capital of the neighboring republic — to which he fled twice. There, in the course of his first escape, he turned into such an avid cyclist that he rode the narrow streets of the old part of the city as even professionals on sports bicycles could not on a cycle track. To the envy of those pseudo-professionals, he even replaced the saddle of his *Десна-два* with the more comfortable seat of the fabulous *Тахион*[3], participated

---

[2] Ноль-шесть (Russ.) – zero six - a short form standing for the Soviet car "Lada 2106"

[3] Тахион (Russ.) – Tachyon – an extremely light bicycle manufactured in Ukraine

in the city championship, and beat all his rivals one by one and as a group. Although he was awarded only a lifetime disqualification at that tournament, he still won the hearts of half the city and, among them, many a great-looking bird in no way inferior to his Milla, if not even much cuter than her.

When he fled to Tbilisi for the second time, the situation in the city was pretty unfavorable: not only *Десна-два* with a *Тахион* saddle, but also a bike leg sticking out into the street could be easily stolen. Small wonder his precious bicycle was lifted before long, and now, lying lazily on a sofa in front of a TV-set, he recalled the day when he decided that he'd better sell it rather than hand it over to the thieves. Unfortunately, he failed to charm the damned buyer with either legendary stories or the *Тахион* saddle, and couldn't persuade him to pay more than eighteen laris[4], and since he did not want to sell his childhood memories so cheaply, he returned home riding his beloved vehicle. During his refuge, he found shelter on the outskirts of the city, where he resided on the top floor of a sixteen-story apartment building. Having approached the main entrance of that very construction, he discovered that there was a usual power outage, so there was no light in the hallway and no elevator to get him upstairs. However, there still *was* an unbearable stench emanating from the mouth of the garbage chute. He didn't feel like walking up the stairs carrying his bicycle… No, not because he was too lazy or something like that, but because loaded with the bicycle, he would be walking more slowly, inhaling the stench all the while. If he hated anything in the world and if anything reminded him of all the hell he had endured — which he had been trying hard to forget with the help of alcohol, complete inertness, and in a million other ways — it was a garbage chute, or rather its all-encompassing nasty smell which instantly reminded him of all his hardships. So, he left his bicycle at the front door and ran up the stairs as fast as he could. At 8 pm, when the power was back again, he

---

[4] Lari - Georgian currency

went down in the elevator, only to find out that his *Десна-два* and its new saddle borrowed from *Тахион* were gone, and to realize that with the loss of his bicycle he lost every link with his relatively pleasant episodes of the past.

Now, lying in front of the TV-set, he recalled it only because *San Antonio* was losing to the *Clippers* on its home court, and Genna again was losing in the sweepstakes his eighteen laris — those sacred eighteen laris that meant nothing to someone, but for Genna it was the money with which he could buy two packs of tobacco and half a kilogram of gingerbread.

07:45

Losing eight kilos in three months at the age of forty-six is really cool, especially if you never in your life have trained in a fitness club or gym. But these *ни то чтобы очень, но все же*[5] flabby arms and thighs are very nerve-racking! *Слава богу*[6], at least her boobs did not sag after breast-feeding two children, particularly after Lazare[7] whom she suckled until he was two and a half years old…He was not yet called *Lazare* back then, and neither was Genna so profoundly religious either, and despite the fact that he had already turned into his own ghost, his wife's life was still tolerable: at least he would never forget to wish her a happy birthday. By the way, it's her birthday today, but Genna is not likely to congratulate her on the occasion… No, not because he has forgotten the date, he just completely rejected all dates that remind him of some hellish events. Naturally, poor Milla cannot be held responsible for the fact that she was born on the ninth of April, and that they also got married on the ninth of April, and even more so for the fact that General Rodionov, again on the ninth of April, attacked protesters on the central avenue of Tbilisi, poisoned them with a toxic gas,

---

[5] Не то чтобы очень, но все же (Russ.) – Not-that-much-but-still

[6] Слава богу (Russ.) – Thank God

[7] Lazare – Georgian equivalent of Biblical Lazarus.

and killed a lot of people with military spades. Moreover, she is not at all responsible for the fact that the ninth of April reminds Genna of Black January, when 130 peaceful Azerbaijani citizens were shot, and that remembering that Black Saturday, he recalls the endless Karabakh conflict which began in 1988 and is still ongoing. Neither is she guilty of the fact that Genna, not able to endure all this atrocity, was broken down and lost, and that the man she loved was trapped under the rubble of the collapsed Soviet Union, and that afterwards, many years later, he left the service in the police, and that the State Prize and Pension for Heroism lost their value along with the devaluation of the local currency, and that their family no longer had anything to sell or take to the pawnshop.

Milla looked at her husband and asked: "*Долго ты так собираешься?*"[8]

And not getting an acceptable answer, she accepted the reality, took responsibility for the well-being of her household, took a hair clipper out of her dowry chest, went out into the street and started working in the first barbershop she came across. She could not cut hair very skillfully, but she could skillfully lean her magnificent breasts against her customers' heads or near their noses, whispering in their ears in a gentle and voluptuous voice. Although she only touched on everyday topics, it was still perceived as flirting, and since she was a woman, and a stunning one at that, the number of her customers grew exponentially. Normally, any new male with messy hair was supposed to make the overly jealous Genna furious... But no! He remained silent, and when he didn't, he drank, recalling the Baku-Yerevan-Tbilisi road and all the shit, hell and corpses he came across, while poor Milla was impatiently waiting for the day when her husband wouldn't be able to endure the sight of all those males standing at the barbershop with flowers and chocolates, and do something—anything, be it attacking his rivals or his wife! But no! Genna kept silent, and when he

---

[8] Долго ты так собираешся? (Russ.) – How long are you going to sit back?

didn't, he drank, recalling all the pain, each bullet fired and gre-nade blasted. He drank and drank and drank until he could do nothing but crawl to his sofa. So, in the end Milla gave up: she stopped messing with him, but she never messed around with other men either... No, not because she didn't want to, her body didn't demand it, there wasn't a long line of men waiting for her, or just because she was afraid; simply none of the men could ever compare with her Genna, who collapsed along with the So-viet Union and turned into his own ghost. As for Mamuka...

Well, Mamuka achieved everything that Milla expected Genna to achieve: he was successful, wealthy, with a mouth-ful of teeth and a sweet smile; he had his own business, a lot of money, and a strong desire to spend that money on gifts for Milla. And despite the fact that Milla had long been tired of looking for Genna's unrealized potential in other men, she still spoke to Mamuka in a different way, smiled at him differently and — no longer touching on everyday topics while whispering into his ear — touched *him*, stroked his hair so gently with her fingers that the poor man hardened and tried hard to hide his erection under a long black barber apron. But Milla still noticed it, and Mamuka, too, noticed something big sleeping deep in this woman, noticing at the same time that only he could awak-en that something. So, he decided to cut his hair twice a month, and he decided to pamper her with gifts, and he decided to give her a membership pass to the fitness club with lots of exer-cise equipment, Pilates and yoga rooms, a swimming pool and a sauna, where he then appeared in front of her wrapped in a white towel and announced:

"Everything you see here, including Finnish pallets, Turkish light bulbs and Georgian water in the pool, belongs to me... Well, I also own ten-times more property and several sports and business class cars, but enough about that; let's talk about what I would like to be mine as well."

"What?" asked Milla.

"You!" answered Mamuka.

And he sat so close to her that it was not the heat coming from the sauna that gripped Milla but the heat of her own body, a sure sign of the beginning of the long and stinging path to the hot flashes of menopause, which she knew were already on the way… But she didn't know how to deal with Mamuka. Although she never in her life had any interest in any other man but her spouse, now her whole body screamed and demanded that she cuddle up to Mamuka, cling to him in the same way as many years ago she clung to Genna while sitting on the back seat of his *Десна-два*. However, throughout all those years she got more and more rational, and damn fears of committing adultery also began to flash in her thoughts… But Milla was by no means an adulteress, though Genna…

Genna stopped sleeping with her after the accident with Lazare. And if she reacted to it with understanding while witnessing how he tortured himself in the following weeks and months, how he suffered going through painful regret as he couldn't forgive either himself or his wife for the passion which nearly caused the loss of their son, a year later she realized that Genna would simply never return either to her or a normal way of life. However, Milla was beautiful: she has always been beautiful both in her youth and even now, with those wonderful green eyes so extraordinary for an Armenian woman, and a very ordinary massive and already muscular ass pumped up in a fitness club; with those stiff boobs of perfect shape and size, and very smooth skin with which she now felt Mamuka's fingers methodically moving above her knee, towards the sacred place; and she also felt his mouth which was looking for her neck, and her chin, and then for her lips while his fingers found what they were searching for… And with the first kiss, all the sexual energy accumulated in Milla over nineteen years flared up at once!

It's common knowledge that nothing can boost men's pride so much as the sight of a woman standing on her shaking knees in front of them and emitting a groan of passion from her lungs. So, proud Mamuka announced with a smile and in a very busy tone:

"One of these days I'll call and make an appointment for a haircut."

But he did not call *one of those days* or the days that followed; he did not even turn up in the fitness club which Milla doggedly visited every day, assuring herself that what had happened was not her fault, that she didn't cheat on anyone and didn't let anyone down; on the contrary, it was Genna who let her down first, and next was her own body. She trusted her logic until a week after the incident in the sauna Mamuka called and said:

"Sorry for not calling you. I was away. What are you doing tomorrow? Are you working or taking a day off on your birthday?"

"Working," Milla answered.

"Your voice sounds strange," he admitted.

Milla remained silent, so he added:

"I'll drop in on you in the evening."

And then she:

"OK."

And then he:

"You have no idea what a wonderful gift I've brought you."

And at that point, Zemma knocked on the bathroom door bringing her mother to her senses:

"Hurry up, will you, Mom? I'm late for work!"

08:24

When Zemma came out of the bathroom, Genna and Milla were already arguing over some trifle. She did not intervene in their argument, she never did. Her parents always, as far as she remembered, have been swearing at each other and attacking each other since they hated each other, but still did not divorce. Was it because they still had passion for each other or were they merely masochists? Zemma did not know, but she knew for sure that she was late for work. So, she asked Milla:

"D'you want me to give you a lift?"

"Машинка для стрижки сломана, мне надо ее починить,"[9] Milla replied.

"So what?"

"Мне надо в мастерскую 'Пиримзе', а это в другом конце города. Я сама дойду, спасибо, дорогая,"[10] and continued to shout at Genna.

And then Genna: "Go fuck yourself!"

And Milla: "I will, 'cause *you* can't do it!"

Each morning starts so heavily for Zemma — with screams, and shouts and yells. But that's all right, she will endure it for some time, say for two or three years at most, till she has enough money to get rid of her parents' hysteria, their filthy apartment building, and its unbearable neighborhood which reminds her of every nasty and horrible experience of the past and poisons her present. Her neighbors, those bastards, steal the windshield wipers of her car or damage its wheels, and they have become so insolent as to even break off the right sidemirror! But it doesn't matter any longer; she is not offended at all; on the contrary, she even seems sort of pleased:

"Попались, суки!"[11] she exclaims and removes a tiny, almost invisible surveillance camera mounted on a rusted gas pipe in front of the parking lot.

Having installed that camera with the permission of the court and in compliance with all laws, she felt, simultaneously, proud and ashamed. She was proud because she would catch the criminals and was ashamed because she also had to watch

---

[9] Машинка для стрижки сломана, мне надо ее починить (Russ.) - My hair clipper is broken, I need to fix it.

[10] Мне надо в мастерскую "Пиримзе", а это в другом конце города. Я сама дойду, спасибо, дорогая (Russ.) - I need to go to the 'Pirimze' workshop, and it is at the other end of the city. I'll get there on my own, thank you, honey.

[11] Попались, суки! (Russ.) – Gotcha, motherfuckers!

innocent people. But what could she do? There was no other way out. When she owned a right-hand drive *Nissan March*, she lived a quiet life, but once she bought a red *Fiat 500*, the situation changed dramatically. Now she'll go to her police department, ask her people to decipher the information, and then she'll make those vandals face the music! Even if the offenders appear to be her next-door neighbors, she will drag them to the police department tomorrow and show them!

Here is what the first paragraph of Article 187 of the Criminal Code says: *Vandalism that results in serious damage is penalized by fines or court-ordered community service from 100 to 180 hours; also by corrective labor up to a year, or house arrest from six months to two years, or imprisonment for a term of one to three years…* Nope, she doesn't want them to be arrested; just a night or two in the bullpen and sentence bargaining will be quite enough for those idiots; and it will be a good lesson for the rest of her idiot neighbors too, who'll guess at last that they better not mess with Zemma! She has the right to keep and bear arms, and if they don't quit that shit, she'll start carrying her gun, and then it'll be worth looking at the faces of the assholes who fool around all day long.

Уроды, достали уже![12]

Zemma showed no interest in terms such as *gender balance, sexual harassment* and *feminism,* or the issues they implied. She came to know their essence much earlier than most emancipated women. She learned from her own experience that all men were rascals, shitheads and scumbags — *сволочи в общем!*[13] Watching her colleagues, she concluded that the majority of Georgian males were very bad fathers, even worse husbands and the most ideal sons for their moms but not for their dads, and despite the fact that 100 percent of them were police officers who work in small departments and have a specific mentality, psychic conflicts and concerns, her conclusion was true concerning any man, including those employed in other fields or even temporarily unemployed.

---

12 Уроды, достали уже! (Russ.) – Freaks, I'm fed up to the back teeth with them!

13 Сволочи в общем (Russ.) – bloody bastards, that is

She would react with a smile to gender harassment, obscene compliments, stupid flirting and genital stock photos messaged over to her. She simply saved those photos and compliments, recorded flirting on a recorder, and sorted all this compromising material in special folders, in order to use them at the right time and in the right situation. She did not stand out with a high rank in her small department, but she showed outstanding firmness and accuracy, and with the help of her stored compromising evidence, she could equally threaten and blackmail anyone, including chief detectives, heads of departments, and even inspectors trained in various frauds.

Apart from all that, Zemma is fluent in bureaucratic Georgian, so no complaint, application or witness testimony is written without her. She became the legislator and pioneer of the trend of long, compound and complex sentences in the police system, as well as the proud author of such intricate phrases as, for example, *to perform regular patrols*, as well as of such reports as *I made a detour in the territory of our action, viz. on the Tbilisi-Senaki-Leselidze highway with a perimeter from eighty-eight to one hundred and two kilometers, which includes the territory from the tunnel of the city of Gori to the turn at Kareli, on which we traveled in an official car, with tail number 4209 and state license plate AF-146 -AF ...*

But Zemma's main merit, which promoted her from a proofreader to the rank of junior lieutenant, is her ability to turn a blind eye to the minor and major transgressions of policemen. Basically, she works with wide closed eyes and doesn't clash with anyone who doesn't clash with her. Now, when she deciphers material with the help of IT specialist Giorgi, investigates a crime for the first time in her life and then succeeds in passing the *standards*[14] in the coming month, she will rise further with a pay rise and, maybe, her loyalty to the system and ability to keep her lips buttoned will be appreciated someday. Besides, a man from the ministry promised to squeeze her into the PR

---

[14] Standards – KSAs necessary for police officers.

department… She just needs a wee bit of support, and she will work her way up herself. She has already managed to rise through the ranks, starting as proofreader and ending as lieutenant, so it's a doddle for her to rise from PR manager to press speaker, and there will be left only a small step to rise from the press speaker up to the minister!

09:30

Genna had a *Zenit* camera, a semi-automatic TTL, and apart from the *Helios* lens, he had a *Super-Takumar* bought at the black market. He also had a *Mir thirty-seven* in his collection, and since he was a jack of all trades and loved to experiment, he dismantled the latter himself and installed its lens upside down. In return for such a hard labor, he received an original image, where everything was clearly visible in the center of the frame, while on the sides the image was reverse, complex and mystically out of focus. Because of this strange and completely unique effect, he fell in love with the *Mir* lens and adored photographing Milla. He mainly used black and white film and took photos of his wife in forests and groves, and the trees in the background twisted and deformed in such a way that an incredibly mystical beauty was obtained. But only the beauty of nature was not enough for Genna, he was looking for something new and original. So, he took one crystal 'drop' from the crystal chandelier that was very trendy those days, attached it to the lens, and in order to get a kaleidoscopic image, he asked his wife to undress. Milla, who was used to undressing and even to *something more* in the most unusual places pretty unexpectedly, immediately undressed in the Gobustan National Park, after which they got not only photographs of extraordinary beauty, but also conceived Zemma. Milla worshiped that day and still remembered all her feelings - how she lay on the cold, cracked ground, and how her whole body cracked with pleasure.

Milla loves to be photographed, adores nudity and aesthetic eroticism. However, in front of the fitness club mirror, she will never stick out her butt tucked in the tightest leggings or put on a sports top that looks suspiciously like a comfortable bra only for the sake of taking a selfie! Neither will she bend over 90 degrees to expose her boobs in a more favorable shape and size. In short, she will never be able to become an Instagram model. Nevertheless, if she posts her photos with #*MILF*, she would receive thousands of hearts, likes, shares, PMs and DMs for which her fellow fitness club members would bust their guts in the literal and figurative meaning of this expression.

Milla always starts her workout with running. The treadmills face the panoramic windows, so she has all the splendor of a long street before her eyes: dirty asphalt, filthy cars, black smoke from yellow buses, people who are already pretty tired in the morning, and a long line of banks, pharmacies, pawnshops, microfinance organizations and currency exchange stalls that involuntarily force a person to switch to something else. But Milla couldn't manage to get hold of a normal mobile phone, so Spotify, YouTube or even pirated copies of music are out of her reach. She can only listen to the radio and then through only one earpiece. But that's all right! Today is her birthday, which, by the way, her family missed: neither Zemma nor Lazare congratulated her. It's clear that her son is still sleeping, but she did not expect such carelessness of Zemma. If no one remembers her birthday, then there is no need to dream of a gift. Well, it's okay... Now she herself will make a gift to herself - she will buy a mobile phone in installments! The only problem is that she is not tech-savvy. All the girls from the fitness club have iPhones, and when Milla asked them what was so special about them, she did not receive any reasonable answer. But from @ *helenofficial* she learned the whole truth: it turned out that a mirror selfie taken by any other phone, no matter how full your butt or boobs look in it, is considered less prestigious, and in the case of HUAWEI even extremely disreputable. Therefore, any Instagram model has to invest money in herself. It's not only mobile phone and fitness club expenses; it's expenses for visiting beautiful places and check-ins, taking photos of delicious food, buying Sunday outfits and good clothes in general. You can't wear the same things all the time, can you? Just imagine dozens of posts a week in different clothes! All those things are not for free, at least in the beginning. Later, when twenty, thirty or even forty thousand slobbering men look at your half-naked, tanned body, companies will bombard you with advertisements; they will bathe you, comb your hair, put lipstick on your lips and paint your nails for free; they will send you to multi-star hotels in different parts of the country so that you also take selfies at the location and check-in, and you should not forget to emphasize which company sent you there. As for travel companies, in the summer they'll send you to the Alps, and in the winter to Mallorca, or vice versa, they don't argue about tastes, you know. In addition, among your forty thousand followers there will be a couple of handsome and rich men who will take you to Paris on Valentine's Day and kiss you if not under the Eiffel Tower, then in the hotel room that overlooks it, and you know yourself what will follow after that, don't you? You're the mother of two children, after all.

"Wait a minute, do you say that Instagram is a new means of getting married?"

"Are you kidding? It has nothing to do with it. When I get married, I am not going to give it up. During pregnancy... Well, I will make vlogs about pregnancy; when I give birth to a child, it will be about childbirth, and then about raising a child."

"And if you break up with your husband, God forbid?"

"Ah, don't you know that the vlogs of single mothers are very popular?"

How can Milla know anything about the vlogs of single mothers? She has managed to use a computer only three or four times! Recently, her boss has been insisting that she learn how to cut women's hair, or at least how to dress their hair. So, poor Milla has been browsing through the Internet for two weeks already to find the right video lessons. For those Instagram girls, it's of course a trifle, but for Milla.... Lazare doesn't even let her into his room without knocking, nevermind letting her use his computer; neither can she use Zemma's laptop for obvious reasons; and at her workplace they have only one antediluvian computer with a square monitor on the rack. So, poor Milla is suffering, while her boss keeps insisting that she doesn't care, but Milla must learn the hairdressing trade! Enough! It's decided - she will buy that damned iPhone today, and she will have one problem less. As for Mamuka...

At that moment, Mamuka enters the gym, bringing with him the fragrance of wealth and a better future. So Milla, who is making a bridge pose and is wearing a gray T-shirt with stains of fresh sweat under her armpits, sees her gentleman upside down and nearly crashes to the floor, but her hero stretches out his hand to her in time and saves her from a bad fall. Feeling his fingers on her sweaty back, Milla is overcome by incredible bliss, and she immediately forgets all those doubts and questions that have tormented her all week. But when she sees his newly trimmed and combed hair, she is seized with such anger that she involuntarily asks him in a trembling voice:

«Ты что, постригся?»[15]

"Yes, I'm sorry, my dear. I had important meetings and I could not go there with a shaggy head, you know ... I assure you that in America it is better to buy a car than to trim your hair!"

"You promised to drop by in the evening," says Milla with heartbreaking sadness.

---

[15] Ты что, постригся? (Russ.) – What's that? Have you trimmed your hair?

"Well, yeah, but when I spotted you in the security camera, I decided to give you the gift right away."

He points to the security cameras, then takes a longish, beautifully wrapped box from his jacket pocket and holds it out to her.

"Happy birthday, darling!"

Neither her husband nor any of her two children remember Milla's birthday, but Mamuka does! Mamuka reminds her of the most important thing in life—that she is a woman, and that she has some feelings and needs… and Milla really wants to hug him … but not here and not now, but in some calm and secluded place under the Eiffel Tower, or in a hotel room overlooking the Tower. Apparently, this desire is so irresistible that it slips into her eyes and smile. So, Mamuka answers with the same smile:

"Get ready, I'll call on you tonight."

Now this is quite unexpected! What did he mean by saying "I'll call on you tonight"? Why would he do that? His hair is already trimmed and much better than Milla can do it, so why would he call on her?

"Just to have supper at a restaurant… It's your birthday after all, shan't we celebrate it?"

Milla, who came out of the shower, stood in the locker room with the Instagram girls, spinning in her memory Mamuka's words: *just to have supper at a restaurant and celebrate your birthday…* Milla's birthday, just two of them, Milla and Mamuka, because that's what normal people do... Or is it what only the rich men do? Nonsense! What does money have to do with that? She would be happy to get a fancy cake or even a small cupcake with a symbolic candle. Is it really that hard? Is it hard to wish your wife a happy birthday? Is it so hard to remember your own mother's birthday? Or is it...

"What did he give you?" asks @*helenofficial* who doesn't know how to help Milla whose head is going to explode from these heavy thoughts, and who's likely to burst into tears … But no, Milla does not cry anymore, because she is used to disappointments and silent sufferings ... Of course, we always feel sorry for those who cry, but a hundred times more we should feel sorry for those who are used to swallowing their tears... Milla opens her beautifully wrapped box and...

"Wait a minute, is it a deodorant? What does that mean? Is that some kind of hint, or what? You should take and shove such a gift up the scoundrel's ass!" says the indignant Instagram Model, accustomed to tourist trips on her birthdays, not even noticing that it is not an ordinary deodorant, but *Impulse*, which Milla observes with such a sweet smile, with which people observe only their favorite sacred things.

10:45

It should be noted that with the blessing of Shaolin and the holy goddesses, Lazare, the same Lazare-Wu, the same Ronin, the same Shaolin's kindred, is a man of rhymes and beats, with *FruityLoops* installed in the radio technology inherited from Genna, and with the head full of new versions in the morning. Today is a PvP day, so he has to rummage around. He's got some great punchlines ready, but he needs some fillers too. He is masterfully gluing rhymes to rhymes:

Like the Messiah I'm living,
Yeah!
Crucifixion is my healing,
Yeah!
'Cause the martyrdom for any Saint
Is a must like keeping Lent,
Yeah!
As for life, it's a terrible mess,
Yeah!
On Tao way it's only excess.

Well, so many 'Yeah-s' sound a bit odd, but the theme is cool. Thanks to Genna, Lazare used to attend a million masses and communions in his childhood, and he formed a peculiar opinion about religion, as he himself explains. He claims that the Church of Georgia left him no other way, since it makes it impossible to be both a thinker and a parishioner at the same time. There thinking excludes being a parishioner and vice versa—being a parishioner excludes thinking. In the end, he himself started preaching everything that he couldn't find in any sermons. In addition, that childhood accident—his baptism by drowning in the bathtub and reincarnation as *Lazare* - also played an important role: willy-nilly, some kind of mysticism leaked from his eyes all the time. Besides, a mix of Wu-Tang, Shaolin Moral, Dao de Ching, and the Way of the Samurai, that is, Asian philosophy and chess thinking, was added to all these, and it distinguished him from all Georgian MCs both mentally and in texts. So, he has no right to lose in PvP. Moreover, he has to knock down any rival in the very first round.

> *I follow the Hagakure Code*
> *And the morality of Bushido*
> *Yeah!*
> *I'm my own judge and priest*
> *And don't feel abatido…*

The beginning is obviously not bad, but he couldn't find a good rhyme for Bushido, other than this *abatido*[16]… Oops, here's a message from work… Yeah, today he will have to vegetate at the Asian fast-food Restaurant '*You* order, *We* deliver', since before 'you order' they must be already there, those Kamikazes on mopeds. They ignore all traffic rules to deliver your chicken katsu and spicy ramen soft and warm. Woe is the delivery guy who cannot move against traffic or has to slow down to let an old woman cross the street on a zebra crossing! Yeah, fellas, if you need to run her over, then do it, and if you need to break the traffic rules, break them! The main thing is to satisfy

---

[16] Abatido (Span.) – depressed.

the customer. You want to be tipped, don't you? So, hey, guys, don't forget to smile!

There are Leftists who have obtained socialist ideas in expensive universities and books, but there are also Lazare-like ones who experience the brunt of the *Concrete Capitalism* first hand. So, Lazare first started to hate billionaires with great hatred, then millionaires, then the business elite, and finally the representatives of the middle and upper middle classes. He hated the middle class, as they were supposed to understand the needs of the Lazare-like ones best, but they always turned a blind eye to their problems; He hated the upper middle class, with their slick hair, manicured nails, expensive perfumes, and dachas bought in the elite places of millionaires' neighborhoods for their passionate desire to get into the clubs of millionaires. All those horrible hybrid formations of the twenty-first century, those who were ruthless towards the poverty-stricken people, were getting on his nerves; He hated when they, with false kindness, a false smile and Pharisee care handed him banknotes with the words: "keep the change for yourself!" Change, huh? Thank you very much, but the fucking five laris is not a change for a delivery guy! Five laris for a deliverer on a moped is the money, for which he, too, has to smile with a false smile; this is the money that Genna needs badly, but he'd rather die than ask his son to give it to him... Genna has run out of tobacco, and there's still a week left before his Pension for Heroism is transferred. He knocks on the door of Lazare's room:

«Яишницу будешь?»[17]

Lazare hated to speak Russian. Armenian was strictly forbidden by Genna, so they did not teach Lazare his native tongue, and Zemma forgot those few words that she knew. As for Genna and Milla, they were never able to learn the Georgian language properly, and despite the fact that Genna blamed the Russians for all the wars and tragedies in the Caucasus, he still spoke Russian, arising the frank indignation of his son. In every

---

[17] Яишницу будешь? (Russ.) – Would you like some omelet?

other way, Genna, fixated on a nineteen-year-old tragedy, was a *what-would-you-like-to-eat-son?* and *put-on-something-so-you-don't-catch-a-cold* sort of perfect father. You can imagine what torture it was for such a father to ask his son for money after treating him with breakfast. But Lazare sensed that something was bothering him:

"What's the matter, Dad?"

"Nothing."

"Nothing" was no longer a reliable answer for Lazare, but Genna was very stubborn - if he didn't want to say something, he wouldn't, and if he wanted, he couldn't be stopped. They were watching TV, footage of the tragedy of April 9th, a chronicle that we recall once a year.

"Were you and Milla already here in 1989?

«*В Апреле?*»[18]

"Yes."

«*Да, уже в Тбилиси жили.*»[19]

"And you didn't go to the rallies, did you?"

«Нет.»[20]

"Why?"

"Zemma was still very little, and I couldn't leave your mother alone…"

Genna was silent for a very long time. He was silent for so long that the whole hell of the nineties flashed before his eyes. Then he somehow managed to raise his head and put his thoughts in order.

«*Никак не могу себя простить… В девяностом даже на митинг поехал в Баку…*»[21]

"Wait a minute, didn't you run away from Baku?"

"Yes, but…"

"And what has happened there?"

---

[18] В Апреле? (Russ.) – in April?

[19] Да, уже в Тбилиси жили. (Russ.) – Yes, we already lived in Tbilisi.

[20] Нет. (Russ.)- No.

[21] Никак не могу себя простить… В девяностом даже на митинг поехал в Баку (Russ.) - I can't forgive myself in any way ... In the nineties, I even went to a rally in Baku.

«Ты шутишь?»[22]

«Нет, я правда не знаю.»[23]

Genna does not like to recall such things, at any rate, he never voices his memories, but Lazare must know that.

"They killed a hundred and fifty innocent people."

"Russians?"

"Of course, who else?"

The politicians did their duty - they laid wreaths and lit candles at the April 9th Memorial. They thanked the fallen for the freedom of the country, and some of them even had a sad expression on their faces. The politicians were followed by the clergy. They held a prayer service for the dead and remarked once again that it would have been better to believe the Patriarch, take refuge in the Temple of Kashueti and thereby avoid the tragedy. This was followed by dry statistics, as if it were not people who were killed with toxic gas and military spades that night but numbers. Then they showed General Rodionov and that was all, no one would remember the tragedy of the ninth of April for the whole year. The program was followed by the mega show *Talents*, which was no longer run on the 'bad channel' where it used to be run earlier, and where one of the participants was doomed to death; now it was run on a channel full of hope, with the same jury but in a new format.

"Now we have an amazing surprise for you - Tsa in the studio!!!"

A disabled girl named Tsa, appeared in the studio sitting in a wheelchair. She rolled towards the center, stopped, got to her feet and, with difficulty but on her own feet, walked to the guest's chair. And the female presenters of the program *Afternoon Show* squealed at the top of their voices, and the only male TV presenter of the same show echoed them.

"Many thanks to the channel full of hope for the fact that it returned the ability to walk to Tsa! Thanks to the power of rebranding and the chief sponsor of the program, the clinic

---

[22] Ты шутишь? (Russ.) – Are you kidding?

[23] Нет, я правда не знаю (Russ.) – No, I really don't know it.

this and this, equipped with hyper-modern technology, which created a miracle and helped Tsa to walk again!"

Lazare finished his breakfast and took the dirty plates into the kitchen.

«Оставь, я помою, а то опоздаешь.»[24]

Lazare thumped his chest twice, made a gesture of gratitude, and was already leaving when Genna overpowered himself and mumbled, dying of shame:

«До моей пенсии пятак одолжишь?»[25]

10:30

The Soviet garbage chute — a stinking mouth of the dragon emitting the smell of decaying food and toxic refuse, a perfect canteen for rats, the evil spirit smoldering like the rotten communist mentality — was afraid of only the Holy Fire! Therefore, Genna would pour the kerosene he could barely get not into his *Turbo*-stove or sticky lamp, but right into the throat of the monster, make a bonfire in its stomach, jump and dance around it, and read Zoroastrian prayers, so that the flame would absorb the all-encompassing stench of filth. A musty smell, black smoke and the soot of bitterness would rise from all sixteen mouths of the dragon, after which it was possible to breathe more or less freely for several days.

The Soviet Union collapsed, it was dismembered and buried giving way to capitalism and privatisation. People privatised everything, including one square meter of the former garbage chutes. They turned that square meter into a storeroom and inspired envy among those who did not have the privilege of living next to the dragon's mouth. Consequently, the coup moved from the city centre to the outskirts, where intense clashes took place on every floor of the high-rises. Despite

---

[24] Оставь, я помою, а то опоздаешь. (Russ.) – Leave it to me, don't be late, I'll wash them up.

[25] До моей пенсии пятак одолжишь? (Russ.) – Will you lend me a fiver till my pension?

the fact that Genna had every right to fight for an extra meter, he did not get involved in those troubles. He would not even walk past the garbage chute, let alone repair a part of it to attach it to his apartment. The stench he felt upon entering the sixteen-story building for the first time haunted him for the rest of his life. First it soaked into his clothes, then into his hair, then into his skin and nails. No soap, shampoo or perfume could free him from the terrible smell pursuing him everywhere. He greatly hoped that by walling up the garbage chute and splitting it up into utility rooms for fruit preserves, pickles and all sorts of junk, the smell would disappear, but his hope failed him just like the hope for earning money betting on some sporting events. All sixteen of the dragon's heads were muzzled, but the nasty smell was still there: the dragon had simply moved into his stomach, and the stink that had vanished from his clothes, hair, skin and nails now slipped through his diaphragm every morning and came out of his mouth. Neither brushing his teeth, nor rinsing out his mouth with mouthwash or homemade tinctures could help him to get rid of that disaster. Small wonder poor Genna himself became a source of stench, since the whole world around him stank incessantly. He tried to fight his own stench as other heroes fought theirs in the mountains and valleys, but they all lost. The old Soviet buildings were repainted in beautiful colors, the ground — with its hundreds of corpses — was covered with a triple layer of asphalt, but nothing could stop the everlasting smell — the stench dominated everywhere.

In the places where street bullies used to hang out near garages set up illegally in the nineties, you can now see football pitches, low-quality slides, seesaws, concrete squares and various other gifts distributed by the city hall before the elections. Every time you pass by them, you remember that you live in a sham democracy; that the bullies have not disappeared but just transformed, still finding common ground with the system. The smartest among them still cooperate with the police, since the government needs the old guard of 'guys in black bandanas' more than swings before the elections. You also remember that fear works much better than social benefits; that the hungry are still scared, and those in need of social assistance receive terror instead. This is how the circle of the sham democracy closes.

Genna was sitting in a community garden set up in front of his house before the city council elections. He was trying to fight back the stench coming from his stomach with the help of a gingerbread cookie. In his cigarette case there were sixteen cigarettes stuffed full of 'German' tobacco, while one cigarette was sticking proudly behind his ear. Just as he was going to smoke it, the hurly-burly at building number eight attracted his full attention. It so happened that he had to stand between the aforementioned transformed bully Noogo and his own next-door neighbor, laryngologist Irakli, and we must admit that he stood between the arguing sides just in time.

"Listen here, cunt! If you park your car here again, I'll fuck your mouth!" yelled Noogo, and it was clear from Irakli's reddened face and trembling hands that his blood pressure increased after such an undeserved insult. But he still tried to keep calm:

"What do you care where I park my car? Have you gone bonkers or something?"

"Wanna screw? You'll drive me really bonkers if you do it again, asshole!"

"*Ты что вообще... Да у тебя же... даже машины нету!*"[26]

Genna tried to grasp the gist of this conflict, but Noogo was not distinguished by consistency, communication skills or logical thinking. However, he had a huge supply of strong words:

"Go, fuck yourself!" he snarled at Genna.

All this might have been another ordinary conflict of an ordinary neighborhood, but nearby, in a black *Land Cruiser*,

---

[26] Ты что вообще... Да у тебя же... даже машины нету (Russ.) What are you talking about anyway, huh? You don't even have a car.

there sat a certain Otar—a resident of building number nine and a high-ranking policeman. Smiling a big smile, he didn't feel like getting involved in the conflict at half past eleven in the morning, but though he was silent at that moment, we still have to remember him, since he can be very useful to us a bit later, in the evening.

12:05

Zemma was born in 1989, while Noogo was born three years earlier - in 1986. In another place and at another time, a three-year age gap would have changed nothing. However, it caused such a great difference in personality characteristics of those born in the late eighties, as if they had grown up not in the same hellish conditions of the same turbulent and painful times, but in two identical though alternative worlds. True, the reality was only one and pretty ugly, but it was perceived in different ways. Zemma was too little to stand in lines for bread, whereas Noogo, together with his mother, fought his way through the crowd, pushing and even weeping aloud to move a little forward. Zemma thought that the Kalashnikov shots were the musical accompaniment of a lullaby, whereas Noogo saw from his window how people killed each other for an absurd or even no reason at all. His father, too, was killed for 1.8 kilograms of expired, moldy pasta from humanitarian aid, a little change in his pocket, and a warm but rather torn jacket... He was killed before his son's eyes...Every morning, Zemma's hair was combed, and colored ribbons were woven into it, while Noogo was collecting non-ferrous metal... and he was not the only orphan doing that: many of his peers had lost their fathers for similarly absurd reasons, so they also sneaked into the abandoned factories on the city outskirts in search of the same metal. Some of Noogo's brothers in misfortune were stronger than him, and others were weaker, and if Zemma smiled at all her classmates and made friends with them, Noogo oppressed the weak and made friends with the strong. Later, the time would surely come when he would be able to oppress all the strong as well, and very mercilessly too. In the elementary grades, he only waved his fists; from the sixth grade he already wielded a knife, and from the tenth he even carried a gun. Unfortunately, Zemma didn't succeed in inheriting her mother's thin waist, beautiful boobs, and sweet voice. However, she succeeded in getting stressed because of the xenophobic tendencies of schoolchildren of the most inexorable age, since they bullied and alienated her for being Armenian. So, she decided to fight for the title of *Noogo's woman*. The struggle for this title was fierce: the girls pulled out each other's hair for it, broke each other's noses, fought with school bags and did such dirty tricks that Zemma could have never imagined. But she had the courage to be more radical than her peers. Despite the fact that Noogo was absolutely indifferent to the spontaneous girl fights in the school corridors or to its winners and losers, he could not resist the sight of the naked tenth-grade Zemma in the school toilet. True, she didn't have a thin waist, sweet voice or beautiful boobs, so what? She had a goal and complete readiness to strive for it. And if in the country, where young women were required to remain virgins till marriage, it was possible to assert herself by losing her virginity, then Zemma was ready to go for it…only not in the school toilet, but in some other place, in a calm and romantic atmosphere. In return, she only needed the whole school to know that the 'Armenian *колобок*'[27], as her classmates nicknamed her, had lassoed the coolest boy in the whole school, if not in the whole district, and got the status of *Noogo's Woman*.

Noogo did not acknowledge her as his woman. He cared for her, protected her, didn't let anyone close to her, but never said out loud that he loved her. So, Zemma would give him as much as unacknowledged women give men, that's to say, not enough, and that *not enough* infuriated Noogo. Zemma

---

[27] Колобок (Russ.) - muffin

knew for sure that he was in her hands and led him around by the nose. She was convinced that she knew him very well; moreover, she knew his hidden personality; she knew that he was a deserter of the war between his good and evil 'I'-s; that he was fed up with cruelty, though had no choice but to be cruel; she knew him sobbing and kneeling before her; knew his most terrible complex acquired in childhood when he had to bathe together with his mom until he was ten; she knew how hysterically he was afraid of women, and that he lost all love wars except the war with her; she knew all his pains, his unstable nature and how to control it whilst not driving him crazy. But she did not know life well enough, and was unaware of the unwritten law of nature: those who you love and trust most, in whose soul kindness and cruelty are at war turning them into mutants or demons ready to swallow you, those you know well or think you do, those you love or think you do, suck out all your energy, destroy you, steal your car's mirrors and move the demon into your exasperated soul.

"It's Noogo!"

On the greenish-black footage taken by the night vision camera, one could see the shapeless body of a man mixed with darkness. Because of the infrared light reflected in his eyes, the pixelated image of the criminal really did resemble some kind of demon.

"Wait, first I have to clean up the frame really well."

"I know for sure who it is."

Zemma guessed from the first glance that it was Noogo - his manner of walking, his gestures...And in general, it was not difficult at all to guess who it was. So, why did she suffer so much? Why the hell did she bother so many people, including high-ranking officials and the judge?

"Who is this Noogo?" Giorgi, the IT guy asked her:

"A neighbor of mine. He was recently released on probation. Oh, how couldn't I guess it right away? Who could it be if not him?"

"If he was released on probation, so much the better! It will be easier for you to drive him back to prison."

"Damn me if I don't!"

13:00

From midday lunches to early fast-food orders, Kamikazes on mopeds, equipped with square, heat-resistant, yellow or blue branded backpacks, pray for you, dear clients, from civil servants to "Basiani"[28] angels: *I serve corporations, i.e. I serve Georgia; I serve Georgia, i.e. I serve corporations!* Hi, from the jungles and ghettos of wild capitalism! How are you? How is your sustainable economy? That's our Shaolin and the Path of Christ, since for us the Saints are those martyrs who keep to a living wage diet. What else can the socially vulnerable, God bless them, worship besides hunger?... But why is the life of the rich a continuous flow, and the life of the poor continuous delivery?

There are, so-called, general and professional observations, as you know. Now these professional observations of things, events and people, in the case of different professions, are very individual and different. If, say, parishioner X is ideal for a priest, since he attends all services and gives very generous donations to the church, he may turn out to be a son of a bitch for people of other professions, such as, for instance, the nanny of his child or the cleaner of his office, because, after buying indulgences in the church, he doesn't pay a monthly salary to them in time, yells at them or, maybe even jokes with them in a vulgar way - who can enumerate a thousand and one ways of humiliating people? Proctologists, on the other hand, observe millions of asses and see the scientific difference between them; they can characterize those anuses in various complex medical terms, but they cannot characterize the people to whom they belong as assholes, at least until the Kamikazes ride their

---

28 Basiani – a night club

mopeds, bypassing all traffic jams in the city with the help of extreme riding, go up to the sixth floor, carrying a huge lunch-box when the elevator is out of order, and, in return, get neither a 'thank you' nor a tip! Yeah! An office employee who orders food every day and says the same stupid words to you: "Sorry bro, I don't have any cash", is an asshole, as well as Lazare's employers who don't block the way for those meanies by adding a tip function to the application! It turned out that the free market has turned ordinary people into slaves, and the logic 'if you don't like it, then quit', has led to the fact that we are only free to choose the type of slavery. Therefore, Lazare, who 'doesn't like it' but 'can't quit', rides a *Honda Today* of 2004 with a damaged security-belt, rushing from one end of the city to the other with chicken teriyaki, and then from the third to the fourth with bar-becues. Of course, he can be like Genna with his principles and 'fuck you' logic, but Genna's is a completely different case: he used to be one of those holy traffic cops who couldn't be bribed and who lived on the meager salary of forty laris. Besides, Genna left the service as a hero and the President's Office pays him three hundred laris monthly. True, this amount is nothing these days, but in 1998 it was considered a lot of money, and he also became a great hero, but more on that later.

Till then, let's simply say that Lazare is to deliver the last order and then have his lunch. Today is a short working day, since on the ninth of April half of the civil servants don't work. Instead of paying respect to the dead and working hard to move the country a bit forward, we rest arranging holidays at the expense of freedom acquired at someone else's expense! So, Lazare will also rest, but only till seven o'clock, that is, till those who still work return home and, having neither a maid, nor a cook, nor slaves and no energy left to cook dinner, order what Lazare will deliver to them after tormenting in queues, overcoming traffic jams and fighting with fellow deliverers. There is something exciting in the fact that during the day you

can look into other people's houses, or rather into the hallways
of those houses, coming up with assumed biographies and life-
styles of the customers. Not all of them are bastards and assholes, after all! The other day, for instance, Lazare met an excellent guy suffering from a terrible hangover in the morning. He
had ordered two hamburgers just to treat the delivery guy with
one, can you believe that? He turned out to be a hip-hop fan
like Lazare and showed him in. He had wonderful vinyl discs
and an excellent hi-fi system, and through its speakers Wu-
Tang was heard in a completely different way and in all the
greatness of Shaolin. Yeah, there are some good guys, and Lazare likes them very much; he likes the fact that you can make
friends with a complete stranger just because you brought him
a hamburger in the morning; he also likes the fact that such
people not only then and there, but also here and today are
friends with him, call him and ask:

"Well, what are you doing?"

"I'm on the go with Kyiv cutlets and Mexican potatoes."

"A terrible match, those two don't fit together at all."

"*You order, We deliver*, but the order itself is your
choice."

"Fuck it, the order! Today is PvP day, remember? You
promised to drag me in."

"No problem. Just come, they're begging people to
stand in the background."

"Fuck your background, I don't mean that!"

" Ah… I see!"

If Lazare is a beginner MC, Pyta, the same Pyta, known
as Pyta, is still in the phase where he is not only embarrassed to
rap in public, but also fails to come up with rapper gimmicks
and MC names. But he is embarrassed not because he is an in-
trovert or a boy full of inferiority complexes, since he is far from
being a boy. Actually, he's already a thirty-six-year-old man,

brought up in the prestigious residential area in the city center, on the money of his parents and grandparents. He has always been a loafer but received his first and second degrees in Europe. He is, in fact, a very deep and interesting person, but prefers to talk rather than do, and if he says that today he will take part in PvP, it means that he is ready to step over the opinion of the elite friends of his mom with a PhD in philology, his daddy's businessmen companions, his childhood buddies from private school, his neighbors whom he befriended later, and many other good, well-off people, as well as over the barbs like "Are you out of your fucking mind? You're too old to be a rapper." But although he steps over all of that, the big fear is still there… Well, it's easy to rap in your home studio, but what about rapping in reality? Is he good enough to rap? Or what will he talk about? Has he seen any serious troubles and pains? What worries Pyta? What is his problem? Maybe only the pricks of conscience because he has never done anything for what he has, and he is so rich that he will never have to do anything?

"Are you sure?" Lazare asked him.

"No, not quite…The moment I told you, I peed my pants.

"Okay then, here's how we do it: I'll deliver this last order and call on you if you're free" … Lazare wanted to say, but he couldn't. At that moment his moped started jerking violently, he lost control, and trying to avoid the car in front, turned sharply to the left, leaned his moped down and trudged ten or fifteen meters along the asphalt until he crashed badly with his head into the garbage bins in the parking lot.

13:15

Apart from the Red Cross and the UN, it was the American Evangelist Church that supplied Georgia with generous humanitarian aid in the late 90s and early 2000s. If the Red Cross and the UN are the organizations that always help fallen countries in any possible way, it's completely incomprehensible what made the Evangelist Church, or rather her parishioners, or more precisely her female members carry out the social program *Evangelist Mothers to the Mothers Worldwide* in Georgia. Sure, we didn't ask them then, and now it's too late to ask. One way or another, they all gave us a helping hand and we grabbed it. If the Red Cross and the UN helped us with bandages, dry food or canned food at best, and other first aid items, in the boxes with beautiful bows sent by the Evangelists, one could also find sweets, chewing gums, pastels, comics for coloring and, in cases of great luck, even hygiene products. The super lucky beneficiaries also got the *Impulse Spice Girls* deodorant spray, and Milla turned out to be one of them. In the early 2000s, when unemployed husbands were replaced by their wives on all fronts, when men began to hate their helplessness and their employed wives respectively, when women, apart from working at two different places, had to do daily chores at home and had no time even for combing their hair and painting their nails, *Impulse* was the only thing that made them feel like women. *Impulse* was a very modern and very significant perfume, a true aphrodisiac that made you love not someone else, but yourself. But how long can one tube of deodorant last? About a month? Two months? Or maybe even three at best. And what after that? After that the period of intoxication with your own body was over and the nasty reality of cutting the hair of unwashed men in order to support your family began. Apparently, then it also so happened that the Georgian Mothers who spoke English established something like their own 'Evangelist Church' secretly from their Orthodox Pastors and Patriarchate, and it is very likely that the female parishioners of these two churches, hoping to get into two different paradises, received humanitarian aid in their churches or even right at home, since they sold beautiful boxes and their content separately. This is how *Impulse* appeared on the Georgian market. So, if you were acquainted with a person who was acquainted with the Mothers who were the friends of the Georgian Evangelist Mothers, you had a chance to buy one tube of *Impulse* for twelve laris, which was not a small amount of money then. But at that time, Genna was already receiving his Presidential pension of three hundred laris, so Milla could afford to feel like a woman herself. She enjoyed this privilege before the *Rose Revolution* and for a year after that. Later, for some unknown reason, American Evangelist Mothers decided that we had become rich enough and stopped sending humanitarian aid. Accordingly, the Georgian Evangelists stopped praying to the 'wrong god' and returned to Orthodoxy. In addition, in the same year, when the door of *Impulse* was firmly closed, the huge doors of the new 'Trinity Cathedral' in Tbilisi were opened wide, so that the grace of God, which stooped in the small cathedral of 'Sioni', could straighten up and float freely in the largest new cathedral in the Caucasus. But even God's grace could not change the fact that *Impulse* disappeared from Milla's life for all thirteen years. As for Mamuka ...

Mamuka memorized every single word that Milla whispered into his ear, and then used the received information in his own favor at the right time and in the right form. So, if earlier Milla needed *Impulse* to feel like a woman, now the name of her impulse was Mamuka! She knew that there were men who would do anything to get a woman into bed, but she didn't know whether Mamuka was really an ideal man or pretended to be such to use her only once and for a specific purpose. On the other hand, what was wrong with someone having a passion for Milla and wanting to make love to her even just once? Maybe it was better that way? But why "maybe"? She knew for sure that it *was* much better! Milla could not decide what she wanted - to be Mamuka's mistress or just to remind herself for a single night that she was a woman. But what would happen after that, when the clock struck twelve, when the fairy tale came to an end, when the carriage turned into a pumpkin and she lost one of her glass slippers? Would she also lose her head, or vice versa, would she find her real self? Did she love her husband? When you ask yourself such a question, does it mean that you no longer love, or on the contrary - do you still love your husband? And if you do, then how can you love someone who has been lying on a sofa in the living-room for almost twenty years? And if you don't love him anymore, then does it mean that you can't betray him, because only the loved ones can be betrayed? But if she still loved him, then she would betray herself... And what if Genna loved her? What was easier - to change Genna or to change herself? Or maybe Mamuka wanted more than a banal betrayal; maybe he wanted Milla not for one night but every night, all of her? No, no, no! She didn't want to change anything; changes are never positive...How she begged Genna not to move to Baku and stay in Yerevan! They used to live at the expense of Genna's parents, so what difference would it make if they received the money via post instead of taking it straight from his parents' hands? But Genna was stubborn like a mule - he kept repeating that he wanted changes, not taking into account that changes are almost always negative ... *Боже мой*[29], How negatively the Soviet Union has been changing lately! How anger increased along with the shortage of food in grocery stores! Those who were called fraternal republics turned into fierce enemies, and those who were Soviet citizens turned into Armenians, Azeris, Georgians, Abkhazians, Ossetians, and began to kill each other according to the Russian playbook written in the nineteen twenties. They first killed each other in the war, and then in the streets; and if at the beginning only the military fired, later ordinary Azeris began to shoot at ordinary Armenians because they were Armenians, and Armenians killed Azeris because they were Azeris, and Samuel ... Poor Samuel! How cruelly he was... No,

---

[29] Боже мой (Russ.)- O my god!

no, no, Milla! Stop and don't think about it! Don't you know that Genna was gutted by those thoughts? You'd better think about *Impulse* and the person who gave you back positive impulses, nothing more, enough of that! Now go to the store and buy a cake, and maybe some liquor too... When you get to work, smile at your colleagues, and especially at your boss. Don't forget you have a client booked in fifteen minutes. Give him a quick haircut and then you're free until three o'clock, so you can go to the bank and get an installment plan on your phone. When you have a new phone, you will watch video tutorials on styling women's hair, your income will increase, everything will be fine, and you will never look back, you will never return to the hell in which Genna is stuck, in which he crashed to smithereens! Enough of that! As for Mamuka... Well, you'll think his matter over and decide on something ... or, to hell with thoughts, just follow your heart!

"Hi, girls!"

And Milla opened the door with her shoulder, as she held a cake in one hand, and liquor and disposable glasses in the other.

"What are we celebrating?" the girls asked, and before getting an answer, one of them was already cutting the cake and the other was pouring liquor into glasses.

"Today is my birthday."

"How can you celebrate anything? Today is the ninth of April!"

Those were already the words of Milla's boss...

Changes are rarely good. She moved to her new workplace last year, in October, and this obnoxious woman has already fucked her up! But she works in the city center and on the main street and makes more money than at her previous job. So, smile, Milla, smile!

"How old are you?" the girls asked and started putting the pieces of cake on the plates, the liquor was already poured into the glasses, and the cleaning woman was already making Turkish coffee.

«*Сорок шесть*».[30]

"Are you joking?"

«*А что?*»[31] asked Milla in amazement, and even more amazed girls answered:

«*Мы думали тридцать шесть или тридцать восемь, максимум сорок.*»[32]

When the cleaning woman poured her coffee into coffee cups, when Milla smiled a kind smile, everyone clinked glasses congratulating her on her birthday and became mouse-quiet getting down to their cakes, suddenly.

"I was there too," the boss said.

"Where?" Milla asked.

"On Rustaveli Avenue, on the ninth of April."

And the woman, who until now seemed to Milla the most insensitive and unemotional creature in the world, began to cry so silently that even her tears were barely visible. The silent sobbing over the experienced tragedies is always identical, and Milla had seen exactly the same silent tears in Genna's eyes, and thank God that at that moment her phone rang - it was Lazare. Apparently, he remembered his mommy's birthday after all. So, Milla took the opportunity and escaped from the boss's tears, otherwise after having been thinking hard, worrying a lot and recalling so many tragic events during the day, she would have burst into tears herself.

"Hello, son!"

"Mom, transfer two hundred laris to me, please! I flipped my moped over and had to go to the mechanic..."

"What do you mean by *flipped my moped over*?" Milla screamed so loudly that even the boss stuck in the eighty-ninth returned to the present time.

---

[30] Сорок шесть (Russ.) – forty-six.

[31] А что? (Russ.) – Why?

[32] Мы думали тридцать шесть или тридцать восемь, максимум сорок (Russ.) - We thought thirty-six or thirty-eight, forty at the most.

"No, no! Don't worry, I'm okay! But if I don't fix my moped, I'm fucked up!

"What's happened? Just tell me, will you?

"Oh, Mom, for God's sake, I have no time for that! Just transfer that damned two hundred! I'll give it back as soon as I get my salary!

13:45

"Just look at these freaks! My name is not Koba Chkadua, if I don't fuck the hell outta them!"

His name *was* Koba Chkadua, and he cursed Chinese workers and the businessmen who, due to some criminal agreements with the government, bought everything on the territory of the Tbilisi Sea[33] except the sea itself, built an Olympic village there, managed to turn it into their own property after the Olympics, and created such a closed commune, where only Koba knew what terrible things were going on.

"These bastards hire Georgians as servants and gardeners, man! Here, in Tbilisi, in Georgia, in our own country they turned us into slaves, man!

«*Кстати, ту девушку вылечили*[34], today they showed her on telly. She can walk already.

"Which girl?"

"The Chinese girl who performed on the *Talent Show* a few years ago. She fell from the cable or was thrown from there."

"Was thrown, my ass! She was a dirty whore, pretending to be a stunt girl…I remember it…I even went to protest."

"Well, I don't know the details, but…"

"Then trust those who know them. By the way, she was a good fucker."

"What do you mean?"

---

[33] Tbilisi Sea – an artificial lake in the vicinity of Tbilisi.

[34] Кстати, ту девушку спасли (Russ.) – By the way, that girl was cured.

"I fucked her."

"Come on! Don't fucking lie now!"

"I tell you she was a whore! She ran a so-called massage-room. Can you imagine what weak and aching backs we must have to open massage rooms every two meters for us, huh?"

"And what dicks do we have that harden every two meters?"

Koba started to roar with laughter, and Genna thought that if our reality is ugly and impossible to endure without embellishment, and if this embellishment is a lie which we often repeat to ourselves and others, eventually we'll believe in the lies we tell, especially if others repeat them too. Probably Koba, who had no education, no job, no past, no present and no future, really hated all the Chinese who worked in Georgia, as he believed that they snatched away his job. However, he would never carry wheelbarrows for the Chinese or any other builders because of his incomprehensible conceit. He also believed that the girl from the *Talent Show* was really a whore and he had fucked her, although of all this, the only thing that might be the truth was the fact that he had really visited her massage room, everything else was a sheer lie - a lie that he himself believed in… But Genna no longer believed in anything, neither in lies nor in the truth. The world in which he used to be living was built on a big lie, and when the time for the truth came, it turned out that it brought nothing but devastation, killing and misfortune. If the lie was a lie for everyone, the truth, unfortunately, proved to be different for different people. There were also those who believed in the veracity of their own lies, and it was then that the line between the truth and lies was erased for Genna, and he finally lost every faith. The only thing he learned was how to distinguish lies from the truth and what was the difference between them.

"Shall we have some beer?"

«Денег нету.»[35]

---

[35] Денег нету. (Russ.) – I have no money.

"I am paying."

"Really? How's that?"

"Let's go, I'll tell you on the way."

And on the way Koba told him a lot of things that sounded true for Koba himself but as the truth can seem different from different points of view, for Genna all his judgments were only bullshit and nothing more. It was sheer bullshit that Georgian land should not have been sold to Iranians and Iraqis; that Turkey wanted to appropriate if not all of Adzharia, then at least the renewed Batumi; that Georgian women should not have married foreigners, and even more so Blacks and Muslims; that the Georgian genes were unique and they needed to be preserved, as well as the Georgian traditions and the Georgian language, because during the second coming, Christ would preach in the Georgian language!

"It is said in Holy Scriptures that *the Georgian language will be buried until the day of the second coming of the Messiah for martyrdom, so that God will speak in this language to all*," proudly announced Koba, and Genna also answered this nonsense with nonsense:

"There are some Georgians who, for example, have American passports, and what shall we do with that? Do you say that even they can't buy the land here?"

And Koba, who was cunning and well trained, answered:

"To be a Georgian you need to have a Georgian soul and not a passport!"

But Genna did not give up:

"And who am I to you?"

"In what sense?"

"Am I Georgian or Armenian?"

At that Koba was taken aback and badly broken. His enthusiasm subsided. True, it was easy to discuss others, but when he had to decide whether his own friend was a Georgian or not, and whether he had the right to buy some land in Georgia, his thread of thoughts broke and all the pearls he had uttered scattered around him like beads. Thank God, one pearl rolled towards a shop and Koba ran after it:

"Give me a two-liter bottle of beer," he said to the shop-assistant. After all, beer was the liquid with which one could fix all the breakdowns.

"What about disposable cups?" Genna asked.

"Let's not drink in the street. We'd better go to my place or yours, or that asshole might pass by, and I'll have to drink with him all night. Yesterday, I couldn't get rid of him until three in the morning, you know what I mean."

By 'asshole' he meant Noogo, and by 'what I mean' all the discomfort that Noogo could create after a few glasses of booze, especially if he was stoned. His morning clash with Irakli proved that Noogo had plunged into some kind of lyrical sabotage and was about to stir up chaos, and Koba wanted to keep himself out of that chaos. If there were sounds of beatings at night, he would close the windows and shutters, and even plug his ears. This meant that he would not come out of his hiding place even if his own brother called him for help. Koba wasn't the only one who was going to do so. The whole area shunned Noogo, and the more people turned a blind eye to street squabbles, the more strength and energy of the nineties the streets gained. Noogo was put in prison in 2007 because of the swastikas on his shoulders and the mentality of a monster, and in 2019 he returned with the name of a martyr with terrible stories about how jailers beat and tortured prisoners several times a day for disobedience or just for fun, and how they staged a cruel show of distribution of prisoners to cells after quarantine. Some claimed that Noogo had experienced even creepier things and pointed, winking to the broomstick[36.] Later, those gossipers were often found with broken limbs or floating in a pool of their own blood. No amount of torment can knock

---

[36] In those years, terrible footage of prisoners being raped with brooms was shown on TV.

the monster out of a man; conversely, tormented monsters become more dangerous, and Noogo had also become more dangerous. He had no money, but he was equipped with weapons and bullets, and hoped to get money with their help. Monsters do not act with the mind, they act with instincts and impulses, and therefore are easy to catch. This is all the easier when the attack takes place at gas stations, where a completely innocent boy, a pump attendant, is killed. In short, Noogo again ended up in prison, and this time for a very, very, very long term, which could not be reduced due to his inhuman torment, pulling out all his nails or even crucifying him filmed on camera and shown on telly...But he was released anyway. So, his neighbors lost all faith in justice and now preferred taking refuge in their own holes to resist chaos.

Genna, who hated all pungent smells, and even more so the stench of old age, drugs, Koba's mother's swollen legs, her dry skin, unwashed hair, and proximity to death, naturally invited Koba to his place. And when they sat comfortably in armchairs, drank a mug of beer, followed by the second and third mugs, Koba's broken thoughts stuck together and

"Genna-jan, you are more Georgian than some of us, and if you are wondering how I get money, I have one good offer for you, so listen to me very attentively."

14:38

On April ninth, two thousand seventeen, at twelve eighteen pm Tbilisi time, A.K. (hereinafter the victim), born in nineteen seventy-eight, ID number zero one zero one zero seven nine three one four two, applied to Shavleg Jokhadze, the detective of the fourth department of the Tbilisi police in the Vake-Saburtalo district. The victim had excoriations...

"What the hell these *excoriations* are?" asked Shavleg Jokhadze.

"The same as scratches," Zemma explained.

"Then what *excoriations* and *excrements?* Write it in a human language!

"A note came from the ministry that all our reports are the same. They demand us not to be lazy and write them in proper wording."

... excoriations in the lower part of the lip, small hemorrhages near the eyes and cheekbones, and an injury on the nose. As A.K. claimed at the interrogation, all the above injuries were inflicted on her on the eighth of April, between ten and eleven pm, by G.G., born in nineteen seventy-five, ID number zero one zero one zero nine one hundred thirty-five and seven..."

"One three five seven."

"Sorry?" Zemma couldn't quite get what was said.

"You've written *one hundred and thirty-five and seven.*"

"Ah, I see. Don't worry, I'll change it at once."

...The incident was witnessed by I.G. — the common child of A.K. and G.G. —born in two thousand fifteen, who cannot be interrogated because of the small age.

I, Shavleg Jokhadze, detective of the fourth department of the Ministry of Internal Affairs, within the framework of my authority, sent the citizen A.K. for examination to the Bureau of Expertise named after Levan Samkharauli.

If the conclusion of the examination proves G.G.'s guilt, we will immediately take further steps.

Prior to the conclusion of the examination, I issued a warrant for the protective order, which will be submitted to the court for resolution within twenty- four hours.

"Thank you so much, Zemma dear! Now, please, write in your beautiful handwriting the testimony of the injured woman too, and that will do."

"If you're going to court, at least put on a tie."

"Ah, sweetie, if I could tie a tie, would I go to work for the police?"

And at this half-true joke, the entire department began to laugh, while poor A.K. stood at the water dispenser and tried to fill a plastic disposable glass with a shaking hand. Zemma came up to A.K. to help her, and the poor thing, trying to cover the bruise on her eye with hair, thanked her.

"The protective order will be ready tomorrow, and if he dares to even yell at you, he will be immediately sent to prison."

"For how long? For a year? Two years? He will kill us as soon as he is released."

Zemma didn't know what to say or what to do. Those victims of domestic violence that applied to police had to endure not only the violence against them, but also had to overcome the public opinion claiming that 'dirty linen should not be washed in public!' Even Our Father, His Holiness and Beatitude Ilia II, Catholicos-Patriarch of All Georgia, said in his sermons that the husband is the head of the family, but he was silent about what a woman should do when the head of the family loses his head, rages like a cursed beast described in *Revelation*, drags her by the hair, swears and attacks her with his fists, breaking her face...What should women do when neither society nor legislation can protect them? The Laws are being changed at such a snail's pace that at present they still cannot prevent femicide, not to speak of sentencing the violent men to adequate punishment. Thank God, Society, Parliament, Church and the majority of poor victims are silent.

"Would you please help me with my makeup? I have a lecture today and I can't show myself to the students like this."

What a paradox it is that instead of arresting the criminal, the police officer has to hide the traces of the crime by putting foundation and lipstick on the face of the victim! The junior lieutenant Zemma Simonyan, who has permission to bear and use arms, has to be silent! Even *she* is silent and tries to hide the horrors of her own past in dark archives of her soul, like cases written off due to the statute of limitations. If crimes can be forgotten because of the statute of limitations, the pain caused by them is everlasting; it always stays with Zemma... She finishes destroying evidence on A.K.'s face, destroying herself along with it. A.K. thanks her and exits toilet, while Zemma remains there, with her own memories, tears and trembling hands. With those trembling hands, she picks up her mobile phone and writes a short text message to the man from the ministry, setting up a date at the usual time in the usual place. And before this time comes, she puts herself in order, deeply inhales her past and exhales her future, once again reminding herself that she can do anything, since only she can be so consistent in cruelty, rational in hatred and merciless in revenge!

In the fourth grade Zemma protested against the ribbons woven into her hair; in the fifth grade she switched to fringed dresses; in the sixth grade she painted her nails; in the seventh grade she started wearing bras; in the eighth grade she began to wear crop tops, and in the ninth — since Genna was given money by the state, Milla also began to work, and the family could afford to dress normally — Zemma put on jeans and then a quite expensive *Helly Hansen* jacket; in the tenth grade, *Kurt Cobain* came into her life and, accordingly, she switched to plaid tops, ripped jeans and *Два мяча*[37] canvas sneakers. When she graduated from high school and went to law school, her taste was finally established, and she gave preference to dress pants, shirts and fitted jackets. Since then, she hasn't changed the style or color of her clothes - black, white, gray and blue... though only dark blue, and only on Fridays.

Now, on a date with the man from the ministry, she takes off her clothes slowly, folds them neatly and puts them on a chest of drawers. Then she takes off her sports bra and very ordinary white panties, and after this routine, mechanical and non-sexual striptease, she jumps with screams of lust into such

---

[37] Два-мяча (Russ.) – 'Two balls', the name of the canvas sneakers that were very popular in the USSR.

a whirlpool of charming and dizzying feelings that can drag anyone too deep. If you can swim in the waves of your partner's body, then you know that if follow the current, you won't be thrown out of the whirlpool. Since men are always splashed out first, the man from the ministry is already lying on his back, moaning and breathing rapidly. But Zemma's pleasure hasn't culminated, so she grabs the man's face between her knees and forces him to dive to the very bottom of the ocean, from where an all-destroying tsunami rises.

When the passion subsides, they both begin to breathe evenly and their hearts beat in the usual rhythm, Zemma opens her laptop and shows the recording of the security camera to the man whom she can neither call her beloved, nor a lover, despite the fact that he begs her to assign him one of these titles, marry him, or just leave him for good. But Zemma can neither leave him nor marry him; she cannot part with him because she loves him, though doesn't admit it even to herself. The man from the ministry is the same age as her father; moreover, he is her father's bosom friend, who used to visit them very often. There is something very beautiful and, at the same time, eerily wrong about the relationship between Zemma and the man, who now seems very pleased and proud, as she has done a good job of research. So, he praises her for it, and adds:

"You don't need my help at all. Tell everything to your boss, so that he calls the district department directly and they arrest this bastard right today."

"I'm not asking you for help, I just wanted to brag to you."

And the man from the ministry beams at her with undisguised admiration:

"I love you, and I'm so proud of you, darling!"

Hearing such praise, Zemma's mood suddenly deteriorates and the smile on her face freezes. Probably it will sound awful, but it's still necessary to comment on the reason for this sudden transformation: Zemma herself does not know why and since when this thought began to haunt her, but ...Well, if it were not for sex, the man from the ministry could be the ideal father she always dreamed of; the father who would praise her and appreciate her heroism and achievements, beginning with her school grades and culminating in investigated crime.

15:08

"You need to make an advance payment."

"Why?"

"That's what the program requires."

"Who?"

"The program."

How could poor Milla know that programs issue demands, and that their ultimatums are backed by loan consultants who are as heartless as police officers? If the latter believe in the power of the law, pray for that law and can calmly send to prison all violators of the constitution, except for colleagues, friends, close and distant relatives, and occasionally even relatives of their wives, then the former — the bankers - can calmly repeat in a kind of prayer that there is no true God except Mathematics, and Figures are his apostles. Those apostles said that the money that Milla considered her salary transferred through the bank was actually a personal transfer from her boss's account to hers. Such transfers were not taxed, and the money that was not taxed was not considered a salary, which meant she wouldn't be able to buy anything in installments unless she paid the bank the advanced payment.

"How much is that?" Milla asked, and she was told that the program required a minimum of ten percent participation.

"That is one hundred and eighty laris, isn't it?"

Milla left home with two hundred and fifty laris. Then there was the cake, the liquor, two hundred laris sent to Lazare and her money was over! Now she wasn't able to not only make an advance payment to the bank, but even take a taxi home! Probably, Lazare would return the money to her someday, but *someday* was an infinite concept...So, goodbye to the new iPhone! It seemed Milla was not destined to buy it. But what was her destiny, after all? Was she destined to support her husband and son—the husband that could be called her husband only symbolically, and the son whose work was also symbolic?

Milla raised Zemma all alone. Genna did not take any part in her studies or decisions when she was in kindergarten, school and university. As for Lazare...

With Lazare it was different. Genna felt very guilty towards his son, and since he had no idea what a good father could be, he decided to become the opposite of his own father. When it was necessary to say "no", he said "yes", and instead of "yes" he said "of course." Despite the fact that Lazare had no idea what oppressed his father and what made him so weak, he perfectly pressed on his painful places and said "I want it" about everything he saw around, and "I don't want it" became just as regular in his vocabulary as the conjunction "and." When he announced that he did not want to wait any longer and wanted a moped, because all his friends and acquaintances had one, and that he would definitely start working and return the money spent on it, Genna said:

"We must buy a moped for the child!"

Only the word 'child' was as inappropriate in this statement as the word 'we', and the expenses of the moped were too much for poor Milla's nerves. So, for the first time in her life, she said a resolute 'NO' to her son's new whim and marveled at her own determination. Therefore, Genna took out a loan with a large interest from a bank and bought his son a moped, ignoring his wife's opinion. But one thing was to buy it, and another was to maintain it and pay for its fuel as the bank took eighty percent of Genna's Presidential pension. So, poor Milla had to buy him even his gingerbread and tobacco at her own expense. For the first few months, Lazare really worked hard and did not refuse to deliver any order. Later, he discovered the Leftist movement, Socialism, began to hate the rich, and found out that he did not like to deliver food to the *loaded* and bow before them. So, he decided to serve only those customers that he liked, who did not irritate him, and in general, it was none of Milla's business how he lived!

Her son very often breaks her heart, but unfortunately or fortunately, Milla forgets insults very easily, willingly forgives both Lazare and Genna, because she remembers well that terrible morning and the previous night, when they had neither electricity nor gas.

Power cuts did not depend on them, but the gas was cut off because of Genna, who refused to bribe the collector and did not want to reset the indicators of consumed cubic meters of gas even though they did not have money to pay the bill. So, while their neighbors warmed themselves by the gas heaters, Milla, Lazare and Zemma had to put on three sweaters and two pairs of socks and sit by the barely burning oil stove. The batteries of the radio were exhausted too, and the silence of their poverty was broken only by the sounds of chugging power generators of wealthy neighbors and screams coming from the street.

♦   ♦   ♦

That day the power was back early in the morning, at about 6:00 am. Milla turned on the heaters, and when the apartment became more or less warm, she pulled poor Zemma out of bed to wash the two-week-old greasy dirt from her head, first with washing soap and then with *Кря-кря*[38] shampoo. When the girl had washed her hair, dried it, braided it, and had toast soaked

---

[37] Кря-кря (Russ.) Kid shampoo 'Quack-Quack'.

in salt water for breakfast, Milla sent her off to school and set about filling the tub for her son, who wasn't yet called Lazare. It was a very smart move — firstly, because the boy loved to splash in the water, and secondly, because in the event of a water outage, which seemed to be one of the favorite pastimes of the democratic government of Georgia after blackouts and gas outages, she would have a supply of water to flush the toilet. Satisfied with her perspicacity, she heated the water with a spiral tube heater, put her half-asleep son into the tub, soaped him well, rinsed the foam down with clean water, filled the tub with toys and went to the kitchen to fill the twenty-liter and five-liter tanks with drinking water. Just at that moment, Genna, who was always pale, unemotional and tired to the bone, came home. His eyes were sparkling strangely, and he was so full of energy that he instantly took his wife into his arms, rushed her to the kitchen, laid her on the table, took off her sweater and T-shirt, tore off her bra, sweatpants and ripped stockings, and began to kiss her with oblivion, just like years ago, just like before fleeing Baku, before fleeing Yerevan, before fleeing himself, and before Samuel's death. He kissed her a lot, and everywhere, and passionately; he caressed her and whispered in her ear how he had always loved her and always would, and asked her forgiveness for being unable or unwilling to express his feelings at times. Now he felt that everything had changed, that his strength had returned to him, and he would become significant. He said that every routine was hell, but there were hellish routines and one of them was Georgia… But even in Georgian hell, his sun would rise, as the night before he had saved the President from death! He said that he and the Minister of Interior Affairs hadn't slept a wink, and that all the high officials of the ruling party and the entire cabinet of ministers thanked him, and all of them, together and individually, promised him the stars and the moon for his heroism, and that soon the time would come when he would be able to fulfill Milla's every wish, when he would give her everything she deserved;

that the time would come when he would start to appreciate himself again, and so would others; that he would achieve a lot, and that he would make his wife happy, and that eternal happiness awaited her. And Milla smiled at him and answered him with groans of lust, and her groans were accompanied by the babble of Lazare, who was left in the bathroom. When the moans grew into rapid heartbeats, Genna began to howl, praising God, earthly Paradise, beautiful Iveria[39], Brotherhood, Unity, Freedom; he praised the homeland that he had lost and that would not accept him back, so now he would take Georgia for his homeland and it would be his fetish. And if Georgia became a fetish, if it was a fetish to lose the truth, and if to live without truth was routine, and routine was hell—then everything that turned into routine was already hell! But Genna still howled, praising the great goals in life! Long Live Love! Long Live Relief and Joy! Welcome Dawn! ...And finally, he ejaculated, releasing from words, praises and howling...Now only the rapid heartbeats of the happy couple were heard in the kitchen, but the child's babble was no longer audible...When the silence from the bathroom seemed too long and unbearable, Genna jumped to his feet and rushed to the bathroom. He found his son half-dead and blue in face, with lungs full of water, and tried desperately for three or four minutes to bring him back to life ... And when by some miracle he saved him, when the child eagerly inhaled the air and returned to life, Genna returned to his usual inertness, locked himself up at home, and announced:

"*Самвел имя проклятое и надо его поменять.*"[40]

So, he re-named his son Lazare...

Milla remembers all this. She knows that if not that unfortunate incident with the child, Genna would move mountains, he would definitely change, he would do everything possible and impossible and achieve success if he had been lucky that one time, but ...

---

[39] Iveria – the old name of Georgia.

[40] Самвел имя проклятое и надо его поменять (Russ.) - Samuel is a cursed name and we need to change it.

Well, what has happened, has happened, and Genna is what he is.

16:16

Georgian men have never stopped evolving. They evolved from homo heildebergensis to homo-sapiens, from homo-sapiens to homo-sovieticus, from homo-sovieticus to homo-tsekhavik, from homo-tsehavik[41] to homo-thug, from homo-thug to homo-street bully, and from homo-street bully to homo-raver. Neither has Pyta stopped evolving. True, he is a Shaolin knight at present, but he used to be a street bully once, standing in the street all day long, eating sunflower seeds and spitting masterfully through his two front teeth. He knew well how and when to prolong the vowel sounds, when to speak in a tense voice and when to cuss. He also knew by heart all the written and unwritten rules and laws of street behavior, and when the written law prohibited standing in the streets idly, and when making friends with criminals became equal with imprisonment, which, in turn, became fatal, when the poor homo-thugs and irremediable street bullies who couldn't change their habits continued their habitual way of life in prisons, the sons of rich parents living in luxurious houses began to travel abroad. Some of those rich young men rushed to Amsterdam because of their love for weed, and some others, who wanted to love not only the weed but also their neighbors, headed to India. They explained everything that happened to them in India by finding the center of the universe, the transition to nirvana, and Goa trance, but we'll call it the transition to the next stage of evolution—loafing, and simply listing what innovations they had to accept and with which they could not come to terms. But first of all, we must here note that they accepted the universe as it was, and even if they didn't like it the way it was, they didn't

---

[41] Tsekhavik – an owner-operator of an illegal factory in the shadow economy of the USSR.

feel hatred for it. They accepted the fact that not everyone who looks straight into your eyes is an enemy, and that you don't need to look gloomy all the time, since sometimes you need to smile, relax and visit clubs where it is dark and you can even dance! Dancing, as we'll see later, played the same crucial role in the development of Georgian men as stone tools did in the evolution of homo-habilis. As for what they could not come to terms with was sobriety. In Tbilisi, it wasn't easy to get even soft drugs, but one could easily get the strongest alcoholic drinks, so the loafers were mostly drunk on vodka and, accordingly, were too aggressive. These aggressive homo-loafers could not accept the truth that others also had the right to live, be free and happy. They accepted the existence of the LGBT society, but they could not accept them in their neighborhood and did not accept the clubs where they could appear. They also couldn't put up with the face-control system of those clubs and their security guys, who got so impudent as to kick them out of the dance floor for some reason, or didn't let them into those clubs at all, after which a terrible swearing and hubbub began. Homo-loafers could not free themselves from their street vocals, so they turned out to be the weakest transitional link in the whole evolutionary chain. But what could be done? Unfortunately, this is how evolution always works — only the strong survive, face their future, and leave their past behind. In the bright future of those strong, a small and beautiful airport was opened in Kopitnari[42]. Just as the migration of the Holy Prophet Mohammad from Mecca to Medina brought Muslims the Lunar calendar, so this small airport brought a new, lunatic life, and created a new species of homo-ravers in Tbilisi. The blessed ones took communion at Berghain and Water Gate, and took so many drugs and powders that the dance demon sleeping in Georgians rose with all his strength and Georgians started dancing. If Georgia is known for anything in the world, it's known for its famous folk dances — the so-called *Georgian Ballet*.

---

[42] Kopitnari – an international airport in western Georgia.

But just as the Georgians were walled up in homo-sovieticus, so the dance was walled up in their bodies. If dancing was only folklore for them those days, and it should be learned how to do it, the blessed ones guessed that in order to dance, one must not learn it, but simply forget oneself and one's own body boundaries; they guessed that dance is boundless freedom, and when a Georgian begins to dance, the Georgian spirit dances too, and it can dance non-stop, till the end of time! The first one in the history of Georgia to guess that was Pyta — the sloshed homo-raver listening to the techno music in the city of Berlin. He felt it with all his soul and let his body into such a self-denying dance that he did not understand how he switched to the elements of *Georgian Ballet* - to squatting, jumping, and tornado-fast spinning standing on the knees. He spun around the entire dance floor and didn't notice how the circle around him expanded, how his audience increased, how a girl jumped out of the audience and joined his performance, how she danced on tiptoes next to him, and how she turned the dance into ecstasy, ecstasy into *Georgian Ballet*, the ballet into the dirtiest sex in a dirty toilet, then again into ecstasy, dance and colossal happiness. It seemed that all the Moiras of Shaolin planned the fate of Pyta this way, and that they knew in advance that he would be dead to the world from an overdose of badly combined drugs, and after several days of being dead, he would have a miscarriage of his old 'I', and a completely new person would be born with only the desire to look again into the eyes of that girl, at least just to ask her what her name was ... But the girl was not at his bedside during his coma days, she wasn't even walking nervously in the corridors of the intensive care unit; neither was she waiting for him near the clinic… Every trace of her disappeared from Berlin, then from Germany and then from the life of Pyta, leaving behind a void.

This void continued until Pyta discovered Ableton Live, and discovered that Georgian dance to techno music in night clubs was more than a love which was found and lost instantly, discovering at the same time that what he was doing in life so far had to merge at this single point.

And a year later, after incredible labor and suffering, a million failures and small victories, he wrote compositions for all Georgian dances. Those were very familiar, but at the same time very original melodies mixed with techno music, and when he was sure that he had created something really valuable, he took his laptop, broke it, and threw it into the river Spree, thus placing it where true art should be, that is, at the very bottom.

Being at the bottom lasted longer than being in the void. To this was added homecoming and realizing that the Georgian spirit is free everywhere except its own homeland. Despite the fact that Pyta spent Fridays, Saturdays and Sundays in the ecstasy of dance and nightclubs, something stifled him, something like a woman's braid entwined around his neck - the braid of the beauty that drove him crazy. And he started looking for her. The more he searched for her, the more he lost hope, and in the end, when he couldn't find his ladylove, he found Wu-Tang Sword and the Shaolin Teachings, and again felt the urge to create music. But now he wanted not only to create music, but also to speak out, to say everything he had been silent about until now. All this was told in the finest detail only to let you know about the biography of Pyta, the transformations that he went through, which will help you to better understand the hidden meaning of what he said: "I know how to find those bastards!" And the steps he took after that. But first, let's clarify that by "bastards" he meant the thieves of Lazare's repaired moped, in search of which he intended to call for the old guard. The thing was that Lazare's sister, Zemma, answered her desperate brother's phone call jokingly:

"Those thieves are definitely some kids who won't get caught anyway, and you won't be able to get back your moped.

Besides, it makes no sense to report the theft to the police - we have five of such mopeds standing in front of our department, but their owners cannot prove that they belong to them. We know for sure that they belong to them, but still, we cannot give them to their owners.

"Why?"

"Haven't you heard about bureaucracy? I understand your annoyance, but there is no point in going to the police - you will be exhausted, and you will also ruin our chief detective's statistics."

"What fucking statistics?"

Lazare could not believe his ears when a police officer advised him not to go to the police, and what was worse, this officer was his own sister!

"Statistics of solved and unsolved cases. Believe me, the detectives hate cold cases most of all, and they will press you so hard that instead of writing a statement, you'll apologize for making them waste time on..."

Lazare hung up in complete bewilderment and desperation, but Pyta was already calling the right people. You can imagine what it was like for him in his own neighborhood, right in front of his house, having a parked moped stolen! In addition, he had to hurry — PvP would soon begin, and he could not allow desperate and demotivated Lazare armed with rhymes to fight in hand-to-hand combat with rivals.

17:58

Школьник[43] and Genna met in 1986 during Genna's first flight. The man from the ministry was 14 years old then and was nicknamed *Школьник* in the neighborhood, since he always had a satchel under his arm, and — according to the law of the genre — wore glasses. He was a typical bookworm who answered

---

[43] Школьник (Russ.) - schoolboy.

questions from the criminal world with quotes from books but couldn't answer the needs of the turbulent time at all. He could not be rude, and he could not oppress anyone. Accordingly, being easy prey, he was easily beaten to a pulp. If not for Genna, nothing would ever change, and with age, his life would have become unbearable against the backdrop of the disappearance of all the products in grocery stores, including smoked sausages, and the invasion of people armed with machine guns. Genna was an alpha male by nature, he had a pure heart, the muscles of Peter Zaev and the mind of Boris Spassky[44]. He understood life well and always had a say in peer affairs. There was something about *"Очкарик"*[45] that he appreciated; most likely the fact that his holy, book-framed world was not corrupted by the ugly reality and gang rules. When Genna felt sad or yawned from boredom, he parted with his neighborhood bullies and paid a visit to *Очкарик*. There he was treated to delicious treats bought with coupons by the caring mother for her dear son, and the dear son, in his turn, treated Genna to Walter Scott and Mayne Reid. He would read books aloud and with enthusiasm to his guest, since Genna could hardly read Russian and couldn't read Georgian at all. But he was a good listener and asked interesting questions to which he received interesting answers from the host. In general, all this and the above mentioned served as good prerequisites for their tender friendship which did not end when Genna returned to Armenia, and even more so when he was forced to flee for the second time and live such a hopeless existence, when, if not for the support of friends, anyone was bound to get lost. In the Tbilisi of the nineties, where they were already wielding not jackknives but Kalashnikovs, terrifying passers-by in the dark streets, Genna's childhood friend somehow coped with the help of his friendship with the right people and intellectual conversations about dramaturgy with the head of the paramilitary organization *Mkhedrioni*. Despite even being dressed up in a military uniform,

---

[44] Peter Zaev (boxer) and Boris Spassky (chess player) – Soviet Olympic champions.

[45] Очкарик (Russ.) – Four-eyes.

he didn't think about military problems and didn't crave to rake in money like the rest, his mind worked at full capacity. The instinct of self-preservation and primal fears forced him to be friendly with the strong, and although he accused himself of conformism, he was comforted by the fact that no one from his circle knew the meaning of this word. They also had no idea about the things he whispered to Genna, showing him the books of Umberto Eco and taking him for a walk around The Prague Cemetery. He often recalled Samuel Johnson's quotes about patriotism, which was the last refuge of the scoundrels, that is, those who had no moral principles and who waved flags, and that nationality was the only wealth of the poor. He also assured Genna that their battle could not be called a civil war for long, because it was not citizens who fought among themselves, but different subunits of the KGB, though citizens might not be able to get out of the water dry. If they were destined to bear the burden of fratricidal war, then Russia would have gotten away with everything as it had done for two centuries.

During these two centuries, only one person in all of Georgia had guessed that the truth is above the motherland, and that it is impossible to turn Georgia into fetish...But what was to be done? If in the beginning was the *Word*, now it was the bullet accompanied by laughter, and the words, as well as ideas, had lost all meaning. It no longer makes sense that the homeland is a unity of individuals and personalities, and not of earth, water, air and fire, although sometimes climate and landscape also shape the character of people. Anyway, these four elements are present everywhere. As for the notion of *Georgians* or *Armenians*—people who think, argue and create the concept of the homeland—the Soviet Union canceled it on the very first day by removing the borders. If a person loses his identity, he loses his homeland. Those who retain their personality and open their eyes, see that people around are blind, and the kingdom of the blind cannot be their homeland. Moreover, blindness cannot be above the truth. If we want to reclaim our homeland, we must face the darkness. Thoughts are born only in darkness, they make us think, and if we think, we'll guess that it is mere masochism to love this homeland in its present form.

◆   ◆   ◆

Indeed, it seemed sort of masochistic on Genna's part to stay where they were surprised and suspicious seeing his ID card:

"Wait a minute, what is an Armenian doing in the March[46]?"

Koba immediately stood up for him saying to the opponent:

"Now look at his citizenship and read who issued this card!"

"Citizen of Georgia, the ID card was issued by the Public Service Hall," the opponent read out.

"See? So, if he is Georgian, then how can he be Armenian?

"He has an Armenian surname."

"If you want to know, he's far more Georgian than you are!" Koba declared proudly and led Genna into the hall where a certain fat man with a huge mustache was in charge of the Congress.

"We must level the Iranians to the ground just as Marwan II leveled us," said the fatty suspiciously resembling Rottweiler's shit and not at all ashamed of his naive ignorance. And while Genna was thinking what might Arab Marwan II have to do with Iranians, the fatty added: "And next we will destroy the Arabs!" hence making it clear how delirious he was. Nevertheless, his words evoked thunderous applause from his comrades-in-arms in this war of madness, after which the fatty 'toastmaster' continued to utter endless patriotic nonsense,

---

[46] The Georgian March – a national-conservative political party, which used to be a social movement known for its anti-LGBT rallies.

thereby confirming that Georgians studied their own history through toasts and speeches made during revelry and feasts, and knew about the terrible incidents of the nineties only by hearsay and word of mouth.

As for the mouth, it can say anything, emphasizing what is beneficial to it and omitting the truth that is disadvantageous. And the truth was that there was nothing Georgian in this Georgian March, and if it weren't for the beer and the feeling of gratitude, Genna would now be sitting in the sweepstakes filling basketball bets ...But he was sitting here, sitting and listening to the stupid chatter of the Congress leader and his comrades-in-arms, and tried hard to understand whether all these people really believed what they were saying, or just pretended to be those idiots who didn't understand that they were all characters of the Russian play written centuries before. Okay, to hell with the naivety of his peers and older people; one could somehow understand their stupid Soviet sentiments and longing for the deceptive Soviet well-being and security in which they used to live, but what happened to the young? What happened to Koba who said:

"There is one more problem, gentlemen. Everything is clear with the Iranians, Iraqis and Arabs, but my friend and I live in the area of the so-called Tbilisi Sea where the Chinese build high-rise buildings, create their own closed zones similar to the Ghetto and do not want to hire Georgians even as laborers...Well, okay, the government doesn't give a damn about us, but at least *we* must do something! How long are they supposed to roam freely on our lands? This is the Tbilisi Sea and not the Beijing Sea, after all!"

This not entirely funny joke caused a roar of laughter. The Chairman of the Congress, who also laughed heartily, wiped away his tears, barely took a breath, and after a two-second pause said:

"You're right, dear Koba, but, you know what?..."

Genna knew that the words before 'but' were doomed to be forgotten, but he didn't know that in a country teeming with elite, even nationalism and fascism could be elitist, until the Head of the Congress went on:

"... first, we need to clear the city center and the embankment district of them, and then we'll look after the suburbs as well. Now we need to make a fuss, and the journalists are not likely to rush to the suburbs."

All this didn't appeal to Koba. He had been angry with more than a billion Chinese all day long and, naturally, 81 million Iranians were not enough for him. But the words of the Leader and the consent of his comrades-in-arms to hit the enemy in the very center still had an effect on him, especially since the Leader made a very flattering offer after that:

"Let's go to a restaurant from here. Then, when drunk, we can beat up some of them if we come across them on the way from there, ha ha ha."

"Ha ha ha," the others echoed as Genna told Koba that he'd rather go home, because he didn't want to go to a restaurant with no money in his pocket.

"What money, don't be stupid! We have lots of sponsors and creditors here."

"Just try to find out if some of them are residing in Russia, bro."

"What does Russia have to do with it, man?"

"Wooooshh, my dear Koba!" said Genna and walked away from the March. The further he moved away, the more he smelled the stench coming from his stomach. This stench always made itself felt when he faced ugliness. And today he has faced too many of such deformities.

18:18

The monthly salary of middle-level civil servants and policemen is only one thousand two hundred fifty laris…Well, there
are some gifts for the solved cases, excess fares, the thirteenth
wages and, in ideal cases, even bonuses. But these ideal cases
are so rare that poor high-ranking officials have to pay bonuses
to themselves, so that they do not have to return the money to
the budget. Hence, they announce those bonuses and even sign
them, claiming that they are exhausted working day and night,
but they would do a hundred times more for their homeland if
the homeland praised them properly. And the state highly val-
ues such people, but never the ones like Zemma, whom it gets
rid of by only some special insurances and such perks as free
travel on public transport and other trifles like that.

Out of Zemma's one thousand two hundred fifty laris,
two hundred fifty go to pay off a loan for a car …Oh yes, she
had no other way out. The thing is that at present, it is impossible to live in Tbilisi without a car if a person wants to emphasize his status as permanently employed. As soon as the bank
agrees to give you a loan, you immediately need to buy a car
and stand in traffic jams for hours. In short, Zemma did exactly
that. If the majority of motorists just drove their cars back and
forth and polluted the already lead-polluted air in the city, then
Zemma needed a car not only because of her status, but based
on traffic logistics. It was impossible for her to get from the
Tbilisi Sea to the nearest metro by minibus, then ride the metro,
and then take a bus to her office. It would be merely wasting
her precious time in vain. Neither could she pay fifteen laris for
a taxi—thirty times fifteen plus fuel expenses would have cost
her more than two hundred fifty. So, she invested her money
rationally. Of the remaining one thousand laris, she spent three
hundred on utility bills and the Internet, and she regularly put
at least half of her free money into a savings account. This was

to continue until the loan was paid off and she had accumulated enough money for the first deposit to purchase a one-room apartment in a new building in the city center. It was not long until then, especially since she was waiting for a promotion and a pay increase. With a higher salary, she could shorten the path to her goal. Zemma had been purposeful since her childhood. In addition, Milla drummed into her from an early age that money is as important in life as happiness; and if you can't buy spiritual happiness with it, then you can buy things that will make you happy. She also told her daughter that the gap between spiritual and material happiness is not at all great, that these two are like two identical pictures, in which only wary eyes can see ten small differences. True, there were happy poor people and unhappy rich people, but Zemma did not have to follow in their footsteps; she could very well be statistically averagely happy or unhappy. In general, when it came to the average, the worldview was always included in the matter: as Zemma had no right to be a pessimist, her average status had to be assessed as happiness, and the only misfortune would be a fall and poverty, which did not threaten her, because true, nature deprived her of beautiful body but endowed her with a mind! It didn't matter that there were those who had both, for they didn't know how to fight, so what they got easily was also easily lost. As for Zemma, she would tightly hold everything that she got with her healthy teeth and would protect it as well as Milla did. Someday, she would probably appreciate her mother's care!

However, we could say that she already appreciates what her mother has done for her and, in return, protects Milla from the bitter truth. For instance, she doesn't let her know that she has an affair with an elderly man who could easily be her father. When the man from the ministry gives her expensive perfumes and other personal care products, she presents them as cheap samples, and buys unmarked white boxes to keep her lies and perfumes into them. Milla, not suspecting anything, is daily perfumed with expensive perfumes that suit her mood, since the man from the ministry buys them just according to this criterion. Milla is only a bit surprised that perfumes in white boxes that are brought to her workplace lose their fragrance by the evening, whereas Zemma's eau de toilettes maintain it for twenty-four hours, or even longer.

As for the samples, the situation is as follows: perfume companies send them in unbranded boxes to different countries and different stores, but they suspiciously end up in the hands of some suspicious people who sell them as 'branded products' much cheaper than perfume stores. This is the kind of scam that both sellers and buyers turn a blind eye to. It turns out that sellers profit by selling samples for twice as much as their real cost, and buyers buy them for this inflated amount, which is five times cheaper than the cost of the original products. In general, the trade in lies suits both parties, since in lies the most important thing is enthusiasm. It's that very enthusiasm that also sounds in the voice of Zemma, who is now listening with 'great interest' to her mother talking to her on the phone about how cheap self-care products bought in her shop—vibro face massagers, face creams, foundation creams, tinctures, sunscreens etc.—rejuvenated her by ten years, and that if Zemma buys this entire rejuvenation kit, then as a bonus, she will be able to visit the company's central office twice a month, where she will be treated to tea, coffee, sparkling wine, liquor, social gossip and deep skin cleaning procedures, followed with rehabilitation procedures with soothing creams, masks with expensive oils and vitamins, and samples for all anti-aging products that will fit her pocket.

«*Ну разве не прекрасно?*»[47] says Milla.

And then Zemma:

"How much is all that pleasure?

«Всего три тысячи лари.»[48]

---

[47] Ну разве не прекрасно? (Russ.) – Isn't it wonderful?

[48] Всего три тысячи лари (Russ.) – Only three thousand laries.

"Have you gone nuts, Mom?" exclaims Zemma, who can no longer hide her indignation.

«Это формула юности, дорогая моя, и потому так дорого.»[49]

"What formula of youth? I'm only twenty-eight, I'm far from getting wrinkles!"

"Everyone thinks so when they are young," Milla insists, and in this insistence one can trace two things: first, that marketing works great, making fools of us through television, the Internet, radio, fear of aging, thirst for rejuvenation, or by sending aging women with an inferiority complex very young and full-fledged girls, who are able to sell you even air, and second - somewhere in the middle of a dialogue with her daughter, Milla guessed that she had been deceived, and that the silver case they wanted to sell to her, and which she would sell to her daughter, didn't actually contain any miracles ... But how difficult it is to admit that you were deceived, as well as to admit to something in general...So, she adds:

"I speak for your good, to save you from my mistake."

"What mistake?"

"Because of using cheap creams all my life, my skin is like a sandpaper."

"What nonsense! I wish I had skin like yours."

"Well, just tell me, do you take it or not."

"Of course not."

"Are you sure?"

"Enough, Mom! You know it yourself that all this is mere bullshit."

Zemma wanted to add something, but her boss summoned her with two fingers and a serious face, so she said:

"Excuse me, Ma, I have to run."

Going to the boss's office, Zemma thought about how she would use handcuffs for the first time in her life, and how she would arrest Noogo — the biggest asshole from her past—

---

[49] Это формула юности, дорогая моя, и потому так дорого (Russ.) – It's the formula of youth, my dear, and therefore it's so expensive.

thereby healing her festering wounds and closing the circle of cause and effect. But first, she had to coordinate all this with the boss, since according to the constitution, she had the right to use police paraphernalia—handcuffs in this case—but she could not carry out the detention procedure. Until now, she often played the role of the police officer who detained criminal young ladies in front of the ministry's television cameras, as the internal police order implied that female criminals were to deal only with policewomen, and Zemma was the only woman in the whole department. By the way, rumor had it that the previous provisional government had made another ostentatious appointment when they hired a policeman solely for his frightening looks—a tall man who resembled a large cupboard due to his broad shoulders and imposing looks—though no one knew for sure how he had managed to move up the hierarchical ladder with his poor intellect and climb into the chair of the Minister of Interior Affairs ... But at that moment, nothing mattered to Zemma as she was concerned with her current problem.

"Zemma, my dear, I've already told Giorgi, and I'm telling you too, that you should erase these records," her boss said, thus greatly perplexing her. She knew it was pointless to ask him why, but she asked anyway.

"Why?"

"There is no other way out. That bastard collaborates with the local branch; you guess what that means?"

Of course, she guessed, she always did, but she never said anything out loud, and that was precisely why she was appreciated. But now, when it came to her personally and for her safety, she did not want to be silent and attacked the boss:

"Does that mean he can get away with it and do the same thing tomorrow?"

"No no! No way! He won't dare approach either you or your car again. They'll take him to the police station today and give him a good lesson. If he bothers you again, I'll show him, I swear on my honor! But now…You know…the elections are approaching… Well…now we even try not to fine the drivers, so… you understand me, this matter also needs to be appeased."

Zemma silently swallowed the rage, aggression and desire for revenge that rose in her throat, and along with the hope for justice, she lost her balance and self-control. The memories of the past, immured deep in her soul, woke up in her. At first, they yawned, then they stretched out and straightened their shoulders, and when they felt that it became very crowded in Zemma's brain, they began to break out of her skull from the inside with all their strength.

18:40

"Georgian rap begins with the characters of Soviet cartoons and the children who grew up watching them. When the Soviet Union collapsed, those children — left without food, electricity and entertainment — took to the streets. It is common knowledge that boys' favorite game has always been a game of war, and since adults raised this game to a higher level by playing it not in the yards but on the main streets, and not with toy guns but with real machine guns, howitzers and tanks, the children, naturally, began to imitate them. As for the difference between children and adults, it becomes as insignificant as nine grams when everyone is holding a machine gun.

The history of Georgia has one peculiarity — it loves to repeat itself, loves allusions and parallels. It so happened that, in both episodes of Georgia declaring independence in the twentieth century, it was armed children who fell victim to the struggle for independence. If in the first episode they died defending their homeland sitting in trenches in the city outskirts, in the second one they died for absurd reasons — for looking unfriendly at someone or simply for thuggish mentality. The first entered history with their names and surnames, and only nicknames remained from the second. Those very nicknames — Big-ear, Curly, Piglet, Sorcerer, etc. — indicate that they were all those poor, embittered children who were left without food, cartoons and a normal childhood life, and took up arms not after their personal wish, but because of corrupted time stuck in incredible chaos. The fact that the first Georgian rappers were called Badzhu, Shurik and Cheburashka, and that in Shurik's first album, the most popular songs were *Hunger, Boy in Hood* and *Crazy with Crazy*, again leads us to a stolen, armed childhood. The album of Bedina, who was arrested for having a weapon, is also called *Weapon*, and despite the fact that since 2000 the situation in Tbilisi has become more or less stable, neither the influence of criminal mentality, nor nicknames created under the influence of cartoons disappeared from Georgian rap. So, we also had Grinch and Pinocchio. If Grinch was a member of the group 'Soldiers for Life' and 'an outcast', Pinocchio was a member of BBC, that is 'Bad Boys' Company'. These two soon began making very high-quality alternative music, but still managed to leave a significant imprint on hip-hop, which in the early 2000s was both very underground and mainstream at the same time. When Deja together with *New Face* sang 'For you, for you, for you the dawn is coming', in his solo career, he also had *Manifesto, Alter Ego* and a unique style. While rap all over the world is very orthodox and religious, where MCs say that "Only god can judge them" or sing for the ideology of the Five-Percent Nation, in Georgia we had *Excessus*, and when in one of their clips the members of that group appeared on the stage crucified on a cross, secularism between rap and our Orthodox Church immediately came to an end — the clergy discovered that they could curse and anathematize rappers, just as they did to rockers. So, this subculture, which was one of the lowest levels in the social hierarchy for the world of thugs, had become a target of bullying. Brave Georgians who listened to Tupac, Wu-Tang and Biggie with great pleasure chased with the same pleasure Georgian rappers, mostly young guys wearing bandanas and durags. Let's here recall the Georgian hip hop girls—Petite Sallo, Squirrel and Big Tiko too, and say that if, according to the thugs, rocker girls were considered easy prey for sexual fun, this kind of a view did not help the rapper girls, and they had to fight for their place, passing through a lot of bullying and wars. Even the recording studios didn't do much for them. At first Georgian hip-hop spread with the help of acquaintances and, popular at that time, cassettes and CDs that passed from hand to hand. But a bit later, the studios *Tbilisi* and *Sano* also began to replicate rap. This was how the Georgian artists became popular due to the stolen beats in which not only the music, but even the length of the songs and the places of the choruses were copied. All this was caused by ignorance of mixing, arranging and a thousand other little reasons. At the same time, few knew about the existence of Busta Rhymes, and, accordingly, that *Bad Friday* by Bone and Graph was also stolen from him. Despite the plagiarism, these two artists are still among the best, and since there are concepts of west and east in Georgian hip hop, they can be considered the avant-gardists of Georgian rap after Kabu and Bedina. A big shout out to Kabu who screams in his *Sisa Tura* and *He Wants You Deep in His Heart* that Georgian hip-hop is back, and for the humor he had maintained even in such an uncouth game as rap! And now back to the 'soldiers by their way of life', the ranks of which, in addition to the aforementioned Bone, Graph and Grinch, were also strengthened by Kado and Gertz. Together and individually, they played a big role in the lives of boys of the 2000s, being it the oppressed or their oppressors. Rap lovers knew by heart the lyrics of the songs *We want to Fuck Our Enemies* and *Who Turned off My Light*, and it was a great joy for them when they saw in the Bali commercial Buka Managadze in the jacuzzi with Hertz, who had his own style and very significant flow. Here, since we touched on the rapper of German origin, let's remember the representatives of ethnic minorities and welcome Fredo — the first and, I'm sure, the last Georgian MC, who rapped in Moldovan; let's say hello to Siyoma, whose address was lost along with the disappearance of the Geo Rap tapes. And since we have also touched on commercialization, we cannot but recall Mamuka Glonti and his projects, as well as Lex-sen, who managed to fill the entire Palace of Sports with listeners even in the 2000s, when thugs were hunting for rappers. Because of his image being too far from the classic rap, his pop songs and excessive popularity, Lex-sen could not become a representative of the underground and could not deserve the respect of easterners or westerners. But he helped to popularize rap. Speaking of the popularization of this genre, we must put up a golden monument to *My Buddies* by Geronimo and *The Wanted*. *My Buddies* is the same for Georgian rap as Coolio's *Gangsta's Paradise* for American hip-hop or *Macarena* for the whole world of the nineties. To make it more comprehensible to the millennials, *My Buddies* is the same as Daddy Yankee's *Despacito*, but with a fundamental difference, since *My Buddies* is high-quality mainstream that opened the way for the Black Prince so widely that he first shot his videos in the brothel *Labyrinth*, which was hiding under the shield of a hotel, and then it came to the point when in those clips he showed half-naked girls. To better understand the situation, you should know that it happened when pop-star Maya Jabua's photo was printed on the back cover of the magazine *Mirror* with the inscription: "Maya will show her navel on New Year's Eve." Now you can imagine when, where and how widely the boundaries of Georgian rap were spread!...Since this speech is already too long, let's take the opportunity to greet with great respect Old Man, who, in my opinion, was the first mumble rapper in the world after Bone Thugs-n-Harmony; let's also greet with great respect the break dancers of *Flying Style*, Joker, Bat, and the whole clan of *The Wanted*, as well as *Diversants*, who probably started rapping as soon as they started talking; greetings to the rappers of *White Nights* too. Those who don't like these guys can kiss their ass! Let those whose names I missed forgive me, since proper respect should be shown to all those who started in the most difficult conditions during the hardest times and brought Georgian rap to this day...In short, I declare PvP open!"

This endless monologue about the basics of Georgian hip-hop was delivered by a special guest who took the initiative to shoot a video clip of the winner. Since this person claimed to be a director and conveyed the history of Georgian rap not only by verbal excursions, but also by documentaries, and also possessed equipment if not of Hollywood level, then quite sufficient for making clips, the PvP participants approved his initiative by hitting their chests with their fists and exclaiming io, io, io! The director introduced to the audience the game rules, which differed a bit from the accepted rules and were valid only for this single case. The difference was that the rivals wouldn't have a beatless verbal skirmish, since there was an invited DJ who, at his discretion, would choose beats beginning from East Flatbush Project, continuing with *Teriyaki Boyz*, and ending with Reggaeton music, and all of them would be sixteen bar beats. So, if the participants wanted and were able to say anything to each other, they had to keep within these sixteen bars. PvP rules made it possible for opponents to hit each other in the face and above the belt, insult the opponent and make fun of his girlfriend, but forbade swearing and hitting below the belt. So, the DJ started his first beat for a warm up, the rotating drum was spun, and the fact that Pyta's name came up first and the name 'Maradona of rhythmic battles' second was the biggest injustice in the universe! While Lazare was immensely happy to attend his friend's hip-hop christening, poor Pyta turned pale.

Suddenly the director announced:

"In order not to start with immediate attack, you two had better represent yourselves first."

And Maradona:

"Let the nooby millionaire be first."

As the DJ scratched his beats, so did Pyta scratch his mind, because he was hinted at what he was most afraid of, and he completely forgot all the lyrics and rhythms that he had composed in his spare time. So, Lazare immediately jumped into action:

"Don't panic! Focus on what you wrote last, you must remember it better than the rest."

And Pyta, smiling a sort of terrifying smile, craned his neck and said to DJ:

"Sorry, this is my first time, bro… From the beginning, please."

And then the director:

"Let's cheer up our brother!"

And then the audience:

"Yo, yo, yooo!"

Pyta looked at Lazare:

"You repeat the last words, okay?"

So, Lazare grabbed the second mic and Pyta began:

> *You think I'm known for having much money,*
> *But I have even more of the swag, man.*
> *(man)*
> *I will control all the Vera and Vake[50]*
> *With my beloved MAC -10.*
> *(MAC - 10)*
> *Come on, you bastards,*
> *Come on, you assholes,*
> *Come on, I'm here with Glock*
> *(Glock)*
> *I'm not afraid of them, the cops,*

---

[50] Vera and Vake – the most prestigious residential areas in Tbilisi.

Even if in prison I'm blocked!
(blocked)
Time passes by but the war is still here
A rapper's at war with his kin;
My words are my bullets, I killed many MCs,
Their bodies here rot and they stink.
(stink)
Times now don't reign anymore, as you see
(you see)
It's me who reigns in this PvP
It's me!

"Yo, yo, yo! Look at this nooby, he's gorgeous!" the audience cheered.

And then there came a call from Pyta's chaps:

"We found the bastards; they are small fry and are waiting for you on Sevastopol Street."

So, they had to leave PvP right before it was Lazare's turn to represent himself. When they were already sitting in the car, Pyta confessed:

"I've never been so high, buddy! Let's fuck those bastards right on the spot and come back here."

And Lazare, sincerely rejoiced at the delight of his friend and even more at the prospect of returning his moped, switched on Sadat X's *Come on* in Pyta's huge, sacred and holy black *Jeep*, which could easily rise envy in all the clergy. And happy Pyta:

"I dropped shit like a pigeon…"

And Lazare started to roar with laughter. It was a hysterical, unnatural laugh that a person resorts to when he wants to subside tension, since any street showdown, even with small fry and even with the support of a friend who used to be a thug, always causes tension.

19:10

At seven o'clock, when the beauty salon was closed, the manicurist Mako didn't put away her instruments; she sterilized them again and while the hairdresser Styopa was cutting and styling the hair of the heroine of the day, Mako manicured her and brushed on her nails two coats of the most expensive varnish used only for elite clients. Since Milla had free make-up from the "Formula of Beauty" on her face, she turned from a forty-six-year-old, tired and disappointed woman into the young Milla of the eighties, whose photos Genna used to take diligently, and who didn't yet know that it was not the years that spoiled the facial skin but fatigue. Looking at her reflection in the mirror, Milla realized that she had never liked herself so much and had never felt such an influx of energy and determination. Before leaving home, she spent twenty minutes picking out clothes, but now, for some reason, she no longer liked her plain and loose black dress, which was enlivened only with multi-colored necklaces and large round earrings. She wanted to wear something special, which couldn't be found in her own wardrobe, but could be in the wardrobe of *@helenofficial*. So, since she still had a little time before meeting her lover, and since *@helenofficial* lived nearby, Milla dared to call her fitness club friend and see with her own eyes Helen's bathroom with panoramic windows, a mirror with LED lighting and a huge wardrobe room — almost twice as large as her own bedroom — packed full with clothes thanks to many hearts, likes, sponsors and one rich lover. In short, Milla dressed up and even became a few centimeters taller due to Helen's high-heeled shoes. As for Helen, she was so satisfied with her own creation that she even took out her phone and posted several memorable selfies with Milla on social media.

"You see, generally, I never post pictures taken with more beautiful women than me...well, you know that the good against the backdrop of something worse catches the eye even more. I have a couple of such 'backdrop friends' with whom I look like a prima donna, but since you are a completely different type of a woman, suiting the taste of completely different type of men, this once I will allow such a precedent and boast of a photo with a Sexy MILF like you," admitted Helen.

Sure, Milla didn't know the meaning of *MILF*, however, *@helenofficial* knew that going on a date only in a velvet dress with a deep neckline on the back would not help matters, and that a date was a gravitational field that liked to shift from a vertical position to a horizontal one, and in a horizontal position it no longer mattered what you had on; what mattered was what was left after you took off your clothes! So, since nature had decreed that men preferred half-naked women in erotic lingerie to completely naked ones, Milla was offered to choose the appropriate lingerie from the collection donated to *@helenofficial* by her sponsors. And Milla chose something that would reveal the whole while hiding a half and say much without words, releasing the sexual demon from the body immured in delicate lace.

It's strange, but when you like yourself, others like you ten times more, and Mamuka really likes Milla: he likes her confusion, that she can't look him straight in the eye and looks at the wet streets through the windshield of his car; he likes himself too, sitting next to Milla and turning from a balanced middle-aged man into a loving boy who manages to kiss her thoughtlessly while the car is waiting for the green light to come on, thereby defusing her tension with lightning speed; he likes that the woman answers his kiss and, in the twenty-two seconds remaining before the green signal, she manages to slip her fingers into his hair — what crazy ardor!

As for Milla, she is already enjoying herself in a very expensive restaurant. She really appreciates that Mamuka first seats *her* at the table and then sits down himself. She also likes that he chooses the dishes and wine himself, thereby saving her from the awkwardness. She likes that Mamuka is the personification of politeness, smiles, fun, and self-confidence; that he tells funny stories and projects a sense of someone *who's-doing-everything-well-and-is-always-in-control-of-the-situation*. The only thing she doesn't like is the ambiguity — it's not clear what Mamuka wants…If he only wants to have a physical affair with her, which seems very likely, then why with her? There are so many women around, much younger and prettier than her. Maybe she's just his whim, a fetish, living proof that he is a Don Juan and can do what he wants and with whom he wants; maybe he is a hunter and Milla is his next prey, from which he is going to make a stuffed dummy and hang it by the fireplace; maybe he is a pervert or a sex maniac… Maniacs, as far as she knows, are also smiling like him, and they can also be pedantically well-groomed...Or maybe Milla herself is a maniac, a retrograde who cannot adapt to new circumstances; who cannot enter into a relationship just for the sake of pleasure, or take pleasure in a relationship…There has been such a rapid reassessment of sex that what used to be considered a sacred act has now become as common and frequent as yawning, and sometimes as meaningless as stretching. What does Milla herself want after all — to take pleasure in this one-time date or to give meaning to her life? And what is the point in the relationship with Mamuka? Is she ready to be someone's mistress? If being a mistress means being desired, then maybe she is, but will it be cheating on her husband? Has she already agreed to adultery? She is not in love with this man, so there is no adultery, and if her whole body screams and demands to kiss him, then she is not walking all over herself and her principles either...So, what the hell does she want? Why does she think so much and sip this wonderful drink in small sips like communion wine? Why doesn't she drink it in one gulp? And if she needs to drink the second and third glasses for courage, let her drink them too, get drunk, and partake in her own flesh and blood and in the most natural impulse that she has been holding back for an unnaturally long time… And why can't she tell Mamuka:

"Let's get out of here as soon as possible and do whatever pleases your soul, which is still quite unfamiliar to me…"

Why the hell is she now sitting and listening to silly comments made just to break the uncomfortable silence?

"This is a duck paté. In order to cook it, the geese are squeezed into cramped cages so that they cannot move, and they are fed on various delicacies. The fatter they are, the less they move and the faster their muscles atrophy. And the feebler their meat is the tastier it gets, so enjoy yourself, my dear!"

And dear Milla, who is already captivated by strange thoughts, completely falls into paranoia and identifies herself with that goose—she has also been selected and evaluated by paté potential, her body has been trained and refined in the fitness club for three months in order to meet modern standards before it was brought to the show to feast on it… *Ну и дура же ты, Милла!*[51] What nonsense are you thinking about?

At that moment, her thoughts are interrupted by the waiter:

"Would you like to have anything else?"

"Bring the bill please, we're already late."

"Late where?" Milla asked in surprise, as the only place she was late for was her home. After Mamuka paid off the bill and left the waiter a big tip, which Milla could receive by cutting the hair of five customers in a row, he declared with childish delight:

"I recently finished repairing my dacha. I haven't shown it to anyone yet, I want you to see it first."

Milla adores Mamuka's ability to plan the near future very simply, without any explanation or questions, and without her consent. It was the very skill she liked about Genna; she liked it when her desires were fulfilled until she realized them;

---

[51] Ну и дура же ты, Милла! (Russ.) – You stupid cow, Milla!

she liked that he would involve her in adventures without asking her, because more than anything else she loved adventures... And when Genna realized that adventures could be not only interesting, but also painful, destroying your whole world, all-encompassing, stinking and even sticky, he refused first from them, then from life, then from his wife, and even from his own self. That's why Milla is now sitting in Mamuka's car. She wants to find the peace she deserves for the second and maybe the last time ...There is nothing surprising or indecent in Milla's desire to be happy! She has been like a clockwork mechanism focused on the welfare of others for a very long time. Her children have already grown up and become independent; both work and have their own income and own life; Genna also has an income that is enough to satisfy his own needs; she has already sacrificed herself enough for her family who doesn't even appreciate it. She lost half her life and her youth for nothing, but now she has found Mamuka. So, she can already breathe easy, let no one bother her; no one is interested in her opinion anyway, and why should she be interested in theirs? Let everyone leave her alone, let them not interfere in her thoughts! If they do not leave her alone even in thoughts, then what better thing to expect from them in real life, in her unbearable reality?

19:25

When Genna multiplied the winning odds of *Detroit*, *Toronto* and *Houston* by the two laris he was going to bet, the amount turned out to be so miserable that he decided to add *Oklahoma* to the list. Russell Westbrook had a miraculous season, and maybe he would have done a miracle in Genna's life too; maybe Genna wouldn't have to beg for money from his wife anymore, and maybe he could repay the debt to Lazare.

Genna was standing at the *Sarajishvili* metro station, considering two possible options of getting home: he could either take the bus and walk uphill to his home in the Tbilisi Sea area, or take the metro to the next stop, then take the bus, and then walk downhill to his apartment building. Unfortunately, he chose the second option, otherwise he would not have seen Noogo and his buddies pushing frightened Irakli into the car—going downhill, he stumbled directly upon them.

"Genna, help!" yelled Irakli in a doomed voice.

So Genna rushed to Noogo:

"What are you doing? *Вы вообще с ума сошли, что ли?*[52] he shouted, desperately looking around for help. But all was in vain: not a single soul was to be seen either around or in the building. The neighbors, who used to keep watch from their windows 24 hours a day, now silently hid behind the damned 'crime-proof' metal-plastic windows and pulled down the blinds. As for Noogo, he stubbornly continued to cuss Irakli out, and ordered his buddies to put Genna into the car too.

Everything seemed to be in order in the country: lights were on everywhere, the streets were lit, mobile networks and television were working properly, the police were trustworthy, justice was restored and the patrol policemen rummaged through the streets, between illogically numbered buildings, uttering mocking and humiliating speeches aimed at young people playing in the stadiums or middle-aged men, Genna's peers, sitting on the benches until it was late. It seemed that the State had eradicated both crime and criminal mentality throughout the country. Nevertheless, Genna and Irakli were still sitting in the car, they still had to listen to Noogo cussing them out, and they were still taken to the Tbilisi Sea, where Genna had already been killed once; where he once …

It all started with empty grocery store counters. Hunger is always accompanied by disgust, and disgust by hatred—the 'holy trinity' that inspired both the founding and destruction

---

[52] Вы совсем с ума сошли, что ли? (Russ.) Are you out of your minds?

the Soviet Union. When the Communist Party could not provide food for the population, it fed people with hatred, as with manna from heaven. It so happened that the 'tree of knowledge' planted in the first half of the twentieth century bore fruit just at the time of the destruction of the Soviet Union and brought the war in Karabakh, in Samachablo, in Abkhazia, in Ossetia-Ingushetia, in Tajikistan and in the Dnieper region. People began to eat each other, and Genna, on returning to Baku from Gobustan, discovered that those who would smile at him before the trip now treated him with hostility; he discovered that enmity blinds people; he saw that in Baku they were at odds with ethnic Armenians, and in Yerevan with ethnic Azeri; he saw how two Armenian students were stabbed to death in Baku; he saw how they stoned his and Samuel's Azeri nanny who hadn't lived a single day in Azerbaijan; he saw how Samuel tried to protect his nanny from stones exposing to them his own back; he saw how Samuel, too, could be stoned for treason, and discovered that the 'patriots' used the concept of the motherland in the same way the inquisitors used the word 'God'. And Genna got scared. He was afraid for his pregnant wife, for Samuel, who had gone almost to the point of madness and was planning to go to war with his bare hands in order to peacefully reconcile friendly nations; he was frightened by his own parents who, as it turned out, had been silently enduring everything and hiding their true faces all these years, but now claimed that Karabakh belonged only to them, that it had always been and would be theirs! They also said repeatedly that the enemies had to die, and that the enemies were not only those with whom you were at war, but all other peoples living on your land, and they all had to be eliminated! He was also frightened by the frequent visits of his father-in-law Artyom, who had given him a *Stechkin* pistol before the summons about his death came from the war ...Eventually, he divided all the gold hidden at home into two, took Milla, Samuel and his beloved *Десна-два*, and fled to Tbilisi.

Besides the Zoo and the metro, the Soviet Union also left the Tbilisi Sea to the city, and when the metro stopped working and animals escaped from the Zoo, turning the whole city into a large menagerie, the Tbilisi Sea proved to be an ideal place for burying charred bones...But before Genna and his friends from the *Mkhedrioni* paramilitary organization found Samuel's grave, they had discovered his killers and the ethnic motive for his murder: Samuel was killed because the Bagramyan battalion in Abkhazia...by the Bagramyan battalion[53] in Abkhazia... since the Bagramyan battalion in Abkhazia...But actually, he was killed only because they could kill him. As the pathologist said after the autopsy, the damages on the body of the victim indicated that he was not simply killed, but also beaten, tortured and ironed with a red-hot iron, after which the murderers tied his hands with a rope, tied the rope to a car and dragged him on the asphalt, and, apparently, they also broke his jaw and cheekbones with the *TT* pistol grip...Who knows what happened after that — maybe Samuel was able to run away from the bandits or was forced to run to make a target out of him for shooting practice...? They shot him in the back twice from 15 to 20 meters' distance. But Samuel did not die from bullets or torture, he died from respiratory failure—his lungs were full of water. The pathologist concluded that in the end he was drowned. It was evident from the scars on his legs that they even tied something heavy to the corpse so that it went to the bottom of the sea, but the rope must have broken, and the body rose to the surface. Only after that did the murderers decide to bury him. Hearing all these terrible things, Milla, who had been crying incessantly all week after Samuel's disappearance, began to cry with such a cry which not only dries up all tears, but also turns anyone into their own dummy.

That was why, at the doctor's surgery, Milla didn't notice that the man standing next to her was no longer Genna,

---

[53] The Armenian battalion, which was named after a well-known Armenian general Hovhannes Bagramyan, the hero of the World War 2, fought on the side of Abkhaz separatists being at war with Georgians.

not even his dummy or ghost, but a corpse—the corpse of her husband, an entire fear, more gray and blue than the remains of Samuel; a corpse that left home in search of his friend and returned back as a murderer; she didn't notice that the disappearance of the *Stechkin* pistol and the murder of Samuel strangely coincided in time; she didn't guess that Genna's friend from *Mkhedrioni* had stopped visiting them; she didn't feel the stench that emanated from her husband, and didn't understand why her husband burned garbage in the garbage chute; moreover, she would never understand what her husband felt when he forced one of the bandits to dig up the body of his friend and then widen the grave ...She would never understand that you kill someone not because you are courageous, but because you've lost all courage; she would never imagine how it feels when you're obsessed by the thought that if you let the enemy go today, he'll come for you tomorrow and find you just as you have found him; and if you don't kill him on the spot, he will kill you elsewhere. Genna's psychosis and his loss of courage were completely justified and he fired...first he killed one bandit, then the other, and even shot them in the head to be convinced they were dead. But he could not convince himself that he would be forgiven for this sin, and that no one would try to take revenge on him and his family. Therefore, after Samuel's funeral, he immediately sold his expensive, four-room apartment in the city center bought very cheaply with his father's gold and moved to a cheap apartment in the outskirts. True, it was difficult to explain to Milla why they were running away, but it was even more difficult to live next to the only witness to his crime. So, he fled from himself and from his only living friend to a remote area of the city. He thought that it would be easier for him to breathe there, but no! When he entered his new dwelling, he immediately felt the all-encompassing stench of the garbage chute and guessed that it was not only the world around him that was stinking, but he himself was smoldering and decomposing for his sins, and that those sins and stench would accompany him all his life.

Ten years later, in November 2003, his old friend reappeared. He reappeared with the aim of involving Genna in revolutionary affairs. As if by chance, he took him close to the burial place of those bandits in the territory of the Tbilisi Sea and made it clear that he remembered everything. Earlier, he never mentioned the incident and never bothered Genna, but now he needed his help in return. He said that if his memory served him, Genna was awarded by the criminal government a medal for heroism, and he was also awarded the order of honor by the President himself, so if he now took the side of the revolutionaries, publicly renounced both the government and the President and threw out his awards, he would do a very significant thing for the country. For this, the instigators of the revolution would appreciate his service and reinstate him in the police force as soon as they came to power! At the same time, they would make him not a simple traffic police inspector, but the head of the department, or even appoint him to some post in the ministry itself! Genna laughed, although he did not say that he had no idea where that order was, and that because of that damned medal, he almost lost the most valuable thing in life. He simply pointed his friend—a former member of the paramilitary organization and a newly baked revolutionary—to the grave of the bandits and said:

"Bury me next to them when I die."

But at present, next to them are a yacht club and a swimming pool—favorite places for girls to hang out, so Noogo and his friends are beating Genna and Irakli a little further on, in a thin grove, and Genna thinks that there is some kind of logic in the world, for if he is destined to die, then his killers, without knowing it, have chosen a very suitable place. He also thinks that it's all very funny; it's funny, indeed, to die because of the parking place of someone else's car; it's funny to die because of such nonsense, and it's a shame that this black humor did not end in the nineties. It's logical that the heroes are killed by recidivists, but it's also very funny that Noogo is killing Genna, and that Genna is acclaimed as a hero…That night, he stopped at the obelisk of *Three Hundred Aragvians*[54] only because he wanted to take a little nap in silence on the road blocked by the President's escort. How was he to know that he would have to save the life of the Commander-in-Chief of the country? He was devouring the bun bought at noon and drinking obviously expired smuggled yogurt, which the driver of *ноль-шесть* had given to him as a bribe. Suddenly he heard the sound of the first, then the second and third explosions, doused his faded, blue-lilac police uniform with the yogurt, and trying to understand what was going on, he saw the burning car of the President and heard the sounds of a terrible gunfight from 40- or 50-meters' distance. An armored Mercedes—a gift from Germany—stood right in front of him and Genna didn't know if anyone was still alive in it. His bewilderment lasted only a few minutes, then the car's door opened and a man looked out... No, it was not Shevardnadze[55], it was the Head of the Special State Security Service, Vakhtang Kutateladze...Genna does not remember who was more surprised—Vakhtang when he saw a traffic cop with a pastry in his hand and dried yogurt on his uniform, or Genna who found himself in the middle of a terrorist attack, but he remembers that soon the head of the frightened President also emerged from the car. Genna had witnessed the change of four successive presidents and had seen the scared faces of three of them, whereas he saw the fourth only on TV and then always at knitting or peeling potatoes. He still does not know which is better—a scared president or a president peeling potatoes. However, Vakhtang Kutateladze knew for sure that Genna was the only person who could help him and the President,

---

[54] Three hundred Aragvians – a detachment of the highlanders from the Aragvi velley in Georgia who fought the last stand defending Tbilisi against Qajar army in 1795.

[55] Shevardnadze – Final Soviet Minister of Foreign Affairs in the times of Gorbachev, and the second President of Georgia, who was ousted due to the widespread protests in November 2003.

respectively, and signaled to him to drive over to their car. The shooting continued, but Genna was not frightened and did what he had to. That was not at all because he wanted to save the useless president of a poor country, but people were dying and he could help them. If he couldn't have managed to save his nanny and Samuel, now he had a chance to save these people, and he saved them. Everything else is already a funny story in Genna's funny life, the blackest humor that brought us to the Tbilisi Sea where he is being beaten. Irakli who, like Genna, regularly pays gas and electricity bills, who has never done anything wrong, never hurt anyone and never yelled, is now yelling from pain; and it's also very funny that Noogo cusses him out in Georgian and Genna in Russian. But funnier than that was when Genna discovered that his mobile phone — his decrepit mobile phone with a broken screen and poor audio — had been tapped by the security committee. When in 2007 he was expelled from the militia that was converted into the police force, and then from the traffic police converted into the patrol police, he received a call from former colleagues asking him to join them. They said that they had blocked the main street to show who were real assholes and who were not. But Genna told them that he was already fed up with rallies and was no longer going to take part in anything of the kind. Two seconds later, his old friend — a former member of the paramilitary organization *Mkhedrioni* and now the backbone of the system — called him and said that, first of all, he had to change his phone, since it was hard to hear him, and then warned him not to join any protest marches, especially that day. Although what was shown on TV that very day was not funny at all, his friend's protective gesture sounded like the most vulgar humor. When the government was changed and his friend remained in his post as before, and the system also remained unchanged forever and ever, it could already be qualified as the blackest humor ever from both political and social points of view; the humor that drove the nation into a frenzy and dropped to the level of Noogo's humor. So, Genna could not help laughing, thus angering Noogo and his three homies so much that they left Irakli and began beating and cussing him out in all four voices and eight legs.

20:14

"Earlier, in my day, neither performances, nor films or even TV news started on time, but no one was ever late for the street showdown datetimes — if it was agreed to meet at eight o'clock, everyone was there at eight sharp. We were not punctual in cultural things, but everything was all right in street showdowns. And now here you are — even in this we are regressing!"

Lazare laughed.

"I've always had bad luck with two-wheelers."

"What d'you mean?"

"When I was a child, I had a *Десна-два* and it was stolen too."

"Wow, I had it too!"

"But mine had a fabulous *Тахион* seat."

"What the hell is that *Тахион?*"

"It's a Soviet bicycle too, a sports type. And *Тахион* seat plus *Десна-два* is my father.

"Well, well…can you explain it more clearly?"

"If I start to explain it clearly, I will have to tell you all my family drama, believe me, but I don't think they are going to be that late."

"I learned to ride a bike on my *Десна-два.*"

"Me too, but that asshole stole it from me."

"Who is he?"

"A certain Noogo, my neighbor."

"Come on, let's go and make him give it back."

"Who shall we make to do so, that fucking Noogo?"

"Yes, why not? Who the hell is he not to make him?"

Lazare did not have time to answer, as he spotted the boys heading towards them. There were four of them, thirteen or fourteen-year-olds, dragging the moped with a great difficulty, and despite the darkness and the distance between them, Lazare still suspected that the motherfuckers brought someone else's moped!

The boys leaned the moped against a tree, and Pyta blinked his headlights several times to indicate where they were standing, then rolled down the window and yelled

"Hey guys, get in the car!"

He opened the back door for them, but they looked cynically at Pyta and Lazare.

"That's not going to work, dude," said one of them in such a confident tone and with so much irony in the word 'dude' that Pyta and Lazare immediately guessed who of the four was the leader. The leader's voice broke due to the transitional age, but street vocals were still heard in it. The rest were silent but glaring furiously, while one even stuck his hand between his trousers and long T-shirt, playing a one-man show of an armed thug, pretty familiar to Pyta.

"Do you want adults to stand in the street, or what?" asked Pyta and while asking this question, he already knew what the answer would be.

"The street does not understand age," the gang leader replied, "and I don't know what's on your mind either; perhaps you've come to take a revenge."

"What fucking revenge? I could have a son your age!"

"And would you like it if your son got into a stranger's car?"

The leader of the gang smiled the evil smile that Pyta used to smile very often when he wanted to piss off his "enemies."

As for Lazare, he could hardly hold back a smile because of this absurd situation, stupid dialogue and the boy who pretended to be armed. Anyway, there was no other choice and they got out of the car.

"At least don't make me squat, dudes, I have a meniscus problem."

"My grandpa suffers from the same boo-boo."

"This cynicism is also outta place."

"Wow, how many demands d' you have, hah?—you don't wanna do this, you don't wanna do that...I also don't wanna return this moped."

"I know you don't, but you have to."

"Kiss my ass! It's just that some special people asked me and I didn't wanna refuse 'em."

"Whatever it was."

"That's what it was."

"So, nail it! Roll that fuckin moped here."

Pyta was already getting impatient, but he couldn't beat up these suckers, scold them or call the police, and the dudes knew it and wanted to finish him off to the end.

"Nope, that won't work that way."

"What the fuck is it now?"

"We didn't have time to ride it or have fun."

"So?"

"So, as we're doing you a favor, you should do the same."

"I'll treat you to ice cream, motherfuckers!"

An evil smile now appeared on Pyta's face, but the boy waved a warning finger.

"What happened? Weren't you askin' to stop that bullshit?"

"Wasn't really askin', but beggin'."

"Let it be beggin'."

Pyta couldn't take it anymore.

"Why am I not your age to break your crooked teeth, you lil' penis-blender?"

The 'armed' guy jerked his hand under his T-shirt and stepped towards Pyta, but the leader stopped him.

"Don't tense up, bro, so you don't fart," Pyta laughed.

The 'armed' guy rolled his eyes in anger.

"I'll show you, dick, how to…"

"How to fuck," he wanted to say, but the leader again stopped him. He looked at Pyta and said:

"Why are you making things difficult?"

And Pyta realized that he had lost control over the dormant homo-street bully in him and went too far.

"Okay, sorry buddy, don't hold a grudge against me," he apologized and turned back into a homo-raver.

Meanwhile, the others studied Lazare. One of them even took off his hat pulled over his eyes and exclaimed:

"You're MC Ronin, ain't you?"

Lazare was confused. He was not a very popular rapper and, actually, he was only recognized in the street for the second or third time. And if on previous occasions he had been very pleased and even started boasting of his status, now he did not know what to do.

"Wow, Yeah, of course! I was wondering why his phiz is so familiar," the gang leader slapped his chest twice and showed peace sign to Lazare, who responded to him in kind.

"Ha-ha, see? Earlier we used to try to find mutual friends to solve problems peacefully, but now…It would've been cool if in my time we, too, had had access to YouTube and SoundCloud."

This time the boys smiled a childish smile, and the one who was the first to recognize Lazare said:

"We all know your tracks by heart!"

"Many thanks," Lazare beamed.

And then the leader:

"Can we take a selfie?"

And Lazare:

"Sure!"

And when Pyta also wanted to take a selfie with them, the boys told him politely:

"We'll take a selfie with you separately, can we?"

"By the way, I'm an MC too," remarked offended Pyta.

After the photo session and street debate were over peacefully, the boys rolled the moped standing by a tree to its owner, and Lazare was finally convinced that it was not his old and damaged *Honda Today*, but a new *Honda Click* from last year's release.

"So, is this our moped?" Pyta asked.

"Sure, we didn't steal another one today," the leader replied.

"Wait a minute, do you mean that you steal several mopeds a day?"

"Yeah. Are we supposed to take turns riding?"

"No, of course not, right you are!"

Apart from the fact that *Honda Click* was the *Harley-Davidson* of mopeds, this model was a million times better and more powerful than Lazare's old and damaged moped. Besides, it was actually brand new. The only problem was that the keys were broken.

"Sorry, we couldn't start it any other way. But the contacts are in order. You just need to attach the red one to the blue and it will start."

If the boys didn't steal another moped that day, then Lazare should be looking for other thieves. Neither the police nor the street authorities would be able to help him...This meant that while looking for his moped, he wouldn't be able to work, and if he stopped working, he wouldn't be able to pay the bank, and if he didn't pay the bank, they would not take anything from him, but he would spoil his reputation of a good banking client, and he would never be able to use such services as installments, quick credit, etc....*You order, We deliver...*As long as Lazare was the one who delivered and not the one who ordered, he had to work...

"Come on, Lazare, it's your moped, isn't it?"

How come Lazare's salary was not enough not only for entertainment, but not even for petrol, cigarettes or other basic needs? And that he couldn't dare ask for money from his mother or sister for the hundredth or thousandth time, and that just at such disastrous critical situations, both banks and microfinance organizations remembered him and sent him seductive love messages from future leeches, saying that they could lend him "two thousand laris without any documentation and collateral"? And how was it that the poor and the enslaved were made even poorer? O Lord, if you heed the prayers of our government, businessmen or our nation and save them, then heed the prayers of poor sinner Lazare and help him...

"Cat got your tongue, Lazare? Come on, say something, we're late!"

Come on, Lazare! What would a samurai do if he were in your shoes? Would he ride someone else's horse? How easy it was to write a code corresponding to one's own feudal reality; how easy it was to write the laws that you would never break; how easy it was to talk about temptations until you found yourself in a dilemma...The one who does not commit a sin, does not live, but those who live, sin permanently...what is a sin after all? The priest whom Lazare visited for confession as a child used to say that you are forgiven only for what you repent...

Yes, Lazare repents, or rather, he will repent for what he will say now:

"Yeah...that's...my moped."

20:33

Zemma's colleagues did not stand out with particular cruelty or strong pressure on witnesses and perpetrators. Even in cases of infringing on their rights, when it didn't work out otherwise, they overstepped the boundaries very slightly and beat them so and in such places that experts and lawyers could not suspect them of anything. If in other police departments swearing was common etiquette when talking to criminals, in Zemma's department, they only cursed in front of the turned off cameras. Doing so, they not only defended themselves, but showed that they were not such cannibals as others. But they were all men, and like most men, they also did not understand women or women's problems. Consequently, at the beginning of the year, at a seminar on the law of domestic violence held at the initiative of the ministry, they had a lot of fun. Somewhere in the middle of the seminar, when the speaker said that there is such a thing as sexual violence against a wife, they laughed heartily, and the more the speaker tried to clarify that sex, even with a wife, should be consensual, the more and louder they laughed. Someone even said:

"Don't fuck your wives in strange poses, buddies; who knows, they might even sue you."

When the speaker tried to explain that the Kama Sutra had nothing to do with it, and that violence could be committed even in missionary position, Zemma's colleagues already roared with laughter. One of them admitted:

"Didn't know I was a missionary!"

Someone asked his colleague sitting next to him what kind of a pose this "missionary position" was, and when he answered that it seemed to be a "traditional position," everyone started joking about it and cheered up even more:

"It would be much better to show the Kama Sutra, some kind of porn, or at least the classics of Tinto Brass, as it turns out that people here don't even know basic things."

Suddenly Zemma's boss, who was sitting somewhere in the back rows not even uttering a word and playing the role of a serious person in front of people from the ministry, could no longer refrain and blurted out:

"Poor thing apparently rapes his wife every night but has no idea about it."

This final note was met with general hysteria, firstly because of the absurdity of the situation, and secondly, because good and appropriate jokes from authority always seem a hundred times funnier. In the end, it got to the point that even Zemma, who came to the seminar equipped with printed sheets from the criminal code, couldn't help smiling.

While the police of the Saburtalo district were repeating the law on domestic violence laughing, joking and having fun, exactly at 8:33, G.G. with a staring blank look, petrified face and a bloody knife in his hand, entered the police building and declared:

"I came to confess that I killed my wife."

Everyone froze in amazement and no one laughed anymore. As for Zemma, she sensed such defiant aggression that she was seriously upset. She instantly perceived all the injustice that women experienced, felt all the oppression and mutilations inflicted on them; she realized that despite the laws protecting them, women of any age were always and everywhere—even in the modern, police state of Georgia—completely defenseless; all of them were defenseless against pathologically jealous husbands, defenseless in the dark entrances of buildings with stinking garbage chutes from the early 2000s, defenseless against drunken and maniacally violent lovers who raped them if they dared to refuse them even only once out of a hundred cases... She felt how helpless they were when they wanted to be acknowledged, when they asked their boyfriends to accompany them to the prom, or to admit at least once, without any violence, that they loved them and wanted them, to make love with them without tearing their beautiful dresses, without pushing them with such force that they broke their heads against iron pipes, without pulling their hair out, without spreading their legs apart painfully, without spitting in their faces, without bestiary passion…just hugging them tenderly…

That day, it was Noogo himself who was important for Zemma and not teasing her envious classmates. Despite the fact that he had refused to acknowledge her publicly, she ran away from the banquet on his first order and followed him to the dark hallway to drink cheap vodka. She hoped that he would realize his mistake and, left alone with her, would tell her at last that he loved her, but no! To confess his love to Zemma meant to realize his own feelings towards her, but Noogo could not admit even to himself that he loved the girl he fucked in the school toilet, in the backyard, on the roofs of garages, in an empty stadium, and in dark hallways; he could not admit that he loved the girl he called a whore and recounted the intimate details of his relationship with her to his friends. Girls like Zemma did not deserve guys like Noogo; such guys only fucked such bitches and that was all. And if the bitches refused, guys subjugated them forcibly, by orders, by pushing them with such force that they broke their heads against iron pipes; guys tore their dresses, pulled their hair out, spread their legs apart painfully, with bestial passion, and spit in their faces… Afterwards, when everything was over, guys threw them out into the garbage chute…

Yes, women are defenseless, they can be thrown out, but they are not weak! Neither is Zemma! She keeps a gun in her locker, and its grip can break front teeth very easily…Yes, Zemma is defenseless but she is strong enough, and the four men in the room can no longer stop her; they struggle with her, try to take away her gun and she starts crying; she cries from the annoyance accumulated in her over the years, and it is a pure accident that the safety catch is released during the struggle and the gun goes off... So, it's unfair that the General Inspectorate is going to open a case on Zemma; it is all the more unfair that the boss yells at her and swears at her; how dare he yell at her and swear at her? The fact that he collaborates with criminals will now certainly reach the ears of the right people in the ministry, and we'll see whose General Inspectorate is going to win! And the rest of the assholes won't have to wait too long, Zemma will see to them all! She has achieved everything independently and will achieve ten-times more if she wishes! Imbeciles like them won't stop her! She will expose them all, beat the hell out of them and throw them into the garbage chute, just like she herself has been thrown!

The head of the department, frightened out of his wits by Zemma's new threats and her old, compromising evidence, says that she has gone crazy, she is inadequate, and it would be better if she went home. He suggests talking the matter over tomorrow, in a calm atmosphere. He says that he, too, has been wrong and admits to allowing himself too much. Certainly, it would be better not to inform the General Inspectorate about the incident at all! Besides, he promises that neither he nor the rest of her colleagues will say anything about the shot. Moreover, they will even erase all the recordings from the cameras and fix the hole in the wall. Now the main thing is for everyone to calm down and then make a rational decision together.

As for Zemma, her rational decision is to call the man from the ministry and tell him the truth, that is, the *whole* truth about her life from the eighth grade to now, 8:33 in the evening; the whole truth that Zemma wants to forget once and for all with his help. She wants to forget her past so that she can breathe freely, live a normal life and plan a peaceful future! The man from the ministry will help her, as always; he will help her forget the past and console her in the present. As for the future, he would appreciate if she took him into account. Of course, Zemma will take him into account, she promises, but at this stage, it would be better to take into account that she has to take his request into account. Later, life itself will show what the future holds in store for them…

20:50

No, Mamuka doesn't have a wife, or rather, he no longer has one, but he used to be married — he had three wives…No, not at the same time, of course. The first time he married at an early age, the second time when he was over thirty and the third time not long ago. He broke up with his last wife a few years ago, but it doesn't matter anyway; what matters is that marriage, as such, did not work for him. No, not because his wives were bad or something, it was him who proved to be a bad husband — he could neither be faithful nor a good family man. Actually, if you don't take into account the payment for the education of his children, the expenses for their luxurious travels and their happiness bought with money, you could not call him a good father either. His eldest child is fourteen, with teen problems, bullying and other challenges at school, you know. Of course, he goes to parent-teacher meetings, takes his child to the cinema and shopping, but he fails to have father-daughter conversations with her. The second child is eight…and, yes, umm… did he forget to say that the first child is a girl and the second is a boy? Well, the girl's name is Sisi…Yes, he hates these made-up names, but his wife insisted on it. Those days it was trendy to call children Tamar, Giorgi, or some strange names. Sisi was still all right, it was worse with his second wife — she named the boy Mamuka without the father Mamuka's consent. She justified her decision by saying that she knew he would soon divorce her, and she wanted to have at least one Mamuka next to her. And she was right about the divorce…No, they did not part because of the child's name. Simply, even this example is enough to show how different they were. He has no children from his third marriage. No, not because he can't make children anymore, he's all right in that respect, merely that young girl did her best to get pregnant as soon as she could. Apparently, someone told her that Mamuka took good care of his ex-wives and eternal children. Well, he was aware that his last wife, who was half his age and ten times more good-looking than he was, did not marry him because of his aristocratic profile and low voice, but her too primitive plans and excessive greed greatly annoyed him and forced him to destroy the family earlier than usual. In general, so that Milla knows, Mamuka never lies, but he does not like to confess to adultery. No, not because he is ashamed, he simply believes that by confessing to adultery, you shift the responsibility from your conscience onto the shoulders of your partner, and he is not such a coward. He is not a coward at all; he is strong and free, and always does what he wants. Now he wants Milla. He knows that Milla has a husband, but he also knows that she is unhappy, because happy women do not whisper anything in the ear of strangers...No, Mamuka is not at all going to destroy her family and ask her to go live with him; he will never ask for that. No, not because Milla is somehow worse than his ex-wives; on the contrary, maybe she is better, more interesting and more beautiful than all of them and she is a perfect partner, but Mamuka has already experienced everything — both true love and marriages of convenience and knows that neither of these work. Therefore, he needs neither love nor convenience; he needs something simpler and very pleasant. In short, he wants Milla, and if Milla accepts his rules, she will get happiness, freedom and ease — the three most important things at their age. But now it is important what Milla herself thinks about this, what she feels.

♦   ♦   ♦

Milla has been thinking all day, or rather all two weeks. She is still thinking, thinking, thinking... She can think no longer, especially since there is nothing much to think about. She did her makeup, did her hair, did a manicure, dressed up, even picked up the right underwear, because the bed is an obligatory end to cheating on one's husband. She actually started cheating on him when she agreed to go to that fitness club...Frankly speaking, she doesn't even comprehend what cheating is and how it happened that she had to cheat on either her family or herself... Oh god, she's started thinking again! Enough, enough, enough! She doesn't want to think anymore! It's her who needs Mamuka and not vice versa; she dressed up for herself and not for him! How does it feel? Well…it feels like being a *woman*, and if it is the only feeling that's going to remain from her relationship with that man, it will be quite enough… Did she say enough? Hmm, it will be more than that—it will be the most important thing. Milla and the women of her generation, whose husbands have gone to the dogs, forgot that apart from breadwinners, cooks, cleaners, mothers and their husbands' nannies, they are women, women, women! Women with a lot of other needs besides washing clothes in cold water, working two jobs, and staying alive. And if it is interesting what Milla regrets, then her great regret in life is that she has lost so much time, lost herself and turned into a creature that only exists from month to month, from year to year, from birthday to birthday, though her birthday is even forgotten. Everyone perceives her as a person who puts the interests of others above her own, perceives her as a mother, or as someone who can borrow money, but not as a woman who also has desires, let alone dreams…She stopped dreaming a long time ago. If the bed is the terminal point of betrayal, then the coffin is the terminal point of death, and you die a real death when you stop dreaming! Tbilisi, this puddle of mud, this swamp inherited by the dead from the dead, is the best place where Milla ever happened to live. Cynical, isn't it? How distressful that the generation of Milla and Mamuka had no youth, that they went straight from childhood to adulthood, straight to hell. What can you dream about when people shoot at each other on the streets, break into houses, iron their victims with hot irons, torture them and turn them into cripples? What can you dream about when you have ferocity for breakfast? Maybe about staying alive? No, they did not dream about that, they prayed for it and probably died just then, when half-dead they read prayers — the prayers of the departed...

Ah, sorry, Milla must go to the bathroom, she must splash a little cold water on her face and come to her senses, otherwise she will burst into tears, won't be able to stop crying and will ruin all her makeup... Mamuka claims that she is very beautiful even without makeup though...She needs to find the door on the right in the corridor, the bathroom is right there. It turned out that Mamuka was lucky: he did not live in the Tbilisi of the nineties, his parents sent him to Germany and he was saved...

But what about those who were not lucky and were not saved? Or vice versa, they were unlucky because they were saved? How about Genna? Poor Genna! He was never lucky in anything, neither in life nor in death, although he tried to achieve both. Genna in Spitak, Genna in Karabakh, Genna and death in Baku, Genna and stoning in Yerevan, Genna and the game of war in Tbilisi, Genna and the Black Saturday, Genna and tortured Samuel, Genna a policeman, Genna with almost drowned Lazare in the bathroom, Genna who failed to be a man, husband, father, hero...But she remembers him as a different person. He was also such a Genna who only needed to be lucky once, and Milla would now sit not in front of Mamuka, but in front of him. Alas! Men like Genna are never lucky, and accordingly, women like Milla are also unlucky, since they fall in love with such men, fall in love with their potentialities they failed to realize due to pains, traumas and a million other hardships; they love the fact that despite bad luck, these men survived, and they stay with them while they are dying a slow death; they understand them, never abandon them and sacrifice their lives for them; Milla loves everything that she sacrificed; loves this unfortunate, fallen Genna; loves her past and prefers her stinking husband to the sterile Mamuka.

Mamuka is a gentleman and calmly accepts her decision, calmly starts the car, calmly takes her to work and calmly says that he understands her. He can understand a lot but, in fact, he will never understand women like Milla. He has a completely different past, a different present and future. As for Milla, she is the woman who is now contemplating her image in the large mirror of the barbershop and rejoicing in being a woman, in being still alive and desirable; she is delighted that this is not the end and it's not yet too late. She hopes that the boy she married still lives inside Genna, that the man who saved the president from death lives in him as well. She has sacrificed a lot for him and will sacrifice one last thing too.

21:12

Genna hasn't been killed, he survived, that is to say, he wasn't lucky this time either. Actually, it's not so common to kill people these days. Life has acquired some meaning, so such things as ruining someone's life, infringing on someone, humiliating someone, scaring someone out of their wits, taking away the last hope from people and bringing them to the point where they prefer to die, also acquired meaning. For Genna, death wouldn't be a preference, it would be a logical end, something like the closing of a circle of horrors...*К черту, поздно уже об этом думать, он жив*[56], although a couple of his bones seem to be broken, his head is splitting, and his right knee also buckles—Noogo's buddy hit him with a folding stick, otherwise how would four people cope with two, hah?

"Fucking pussy suckers!" said Genna.

And then Irakli:

""I haven't fought anyone in twenty years."

"Can that be called a fight, Irakli-Jan?"[57]

"Whatever it was."

"This is called lawlessness and a scuffle."

"Anyway, I haven't been beaten for twenty-two years. The last time I was beaten by a thief, and now you see what I've come to."

«А по-моему, один хуй кто тебя бьет.»[58]

"Well, yeah, right you are."

"Was it also for parking they beat you last time?"

"No, no. There weren't so many cars back then. I was operating on a thief's kid, removing his tonsils, and the son of a bitch started crying."

"Did they beat you because of that?"

"What are you so surprised about? Did they have more serious reasons today, or..."

Before he could finish his sentence, a car appeared on the road. They started waving, but who would pick up two beaten, mud-covered passengers right at the cemetery? Moreover, not at the archaeological graveyard of the nineties, but at an illegal cemetery with marble tombstones, opened without the permission of the state? Yes, the cemetery was illegal, since in Georgia, you can't even die without the permission of the state. So, elite dachas or multi-story buildings will definitely grow on the chests of the illegally dead buried there.

"All in all, I learned a good lesson then."

---

[56] К черту, поздно уже об этом думать, он жив. (Russ.) – Damn it all, it's too late to think about it, he's alive.

[57] Irakli-jan (Armen.) – Dear Irakli.

[58] А по-моему, один хуй кто тебя бьет (Russ.) – It makes no difference to me which cock is fucking me.

"Don't you treat thieves' children anymore?"

"Oh, no. I just give the kids pre-op toys — toy guns to the boys and barbies to the girls. And you know what? It works."

"Do they stop crying?"

"No, of course they don't, they are kids and they always cry, but their parents don't beat me."

"I see. And what did you learn today?

Irakli, was broken down, he was scared, he lost all hope…Doesn't violence teach that to us, Irakli-jan? Never mind, we have endured worse things, haven't we? Look, a minibus is coming, you need to wave your hand… Maybe the world has not yet abused this driver, maybe he is naive, a moron, or even worse—a kind person. Wave your hand, maybe he stops…Maybe the driver and passengers are builders from the Chinese ghetto, maybe these Chinese aren't as bad as Koba thinks they are, maybe there are women among them who will clean your wounds with a damp cloth and smear them with some ointment, maybe they speak Georgian and will offer to call the patrol… But wait a minute! Genna notices something in the cemetery…Well, he'll rush there and be back in an instant... What did he find there? It's none of Irakli's business…Genna is back, so Irakli can go now. But he should remember: when he gets out of the minibus, he shouldn't forget to say thank you; he shouldn't forget these Chinese either, and the lesson he's been taught today. Let him park his damn car somewhere far away and not worry that from now on, a huge SUV of a high-ranking policeman will be parked in its place. It can't be helped. This country used to belong to the criminals, and now it belongs to the police, so he can assume that for him and people like him nothing has changed and will never change. Noogo and Koba will always remain what they are: they will drink together every night, and Koba will try to sneak out before Noogo, having taken a lot of alcohol and drugstore rubbish, starts yelling and swearing, and the neighbors start locking all their windows and doors. He must get used to the fact that his neighbors and the whole world around him will never change. Football grounds will be built, cracks will be covered with a new layer of asphalt, entrances will be repaired, but the stench of garbage chutes laid in the foundation of post-Soviet Georgia will still break through. Irakli-jan, can't you smell that stench? Don't you feel that it is still here? That it clung to us tightly like a tick? This stench dries you out, it makes you fade...Aren't your eyes burning, Irakli-jan? Never mind, bro, shed a few tears, cry aloud, but don't break down! No, not because the future has something good in store for you—so far, only the fragile façade of democracy has collapsed, and you've only passed through the first gate of hell. Mind you, it's only the beginning...Get out of the elevator very quietly and don't say anything to anyone, even to Genna, because he already knows what has happened, he has already gone through it and learned a lot; now he's simply revising his lessons, and not for the first but for the hundredth time...

Milla is also asking Genna for the hundredth time who has beaten him and why, but Genna does not want to answer her. However, he wants to wish her a happy birthday and gives her flowers snatched from the cemetery.

As for Milla, she has a plan, Milla is now very self-confident, Milla has not even changed her clothes yet, and she is very beautiful, especially when she undresses for Genna... However, she's beautiful not for him, but for herself, only for herself! She has always been following Genna, so let him follow her now, first into the bedroom and then into their past, when they were still children, when she would cling to him, sitting in the back seat of his *Десна-два*, when she would hug and kiss him, when they had sex for the first time and couldn't part from each other, when they had teeth marks left on their bodies, and when they loved each other to the point of pain; in the distant past, when, during their wedding, they went to the toilet and Genna, diving under Milla's white wedding dress, gave her the strangest wedding gift, and then she knelt in front of her husband, and he let out such a roar of bliss that there appeared cracks on the mirror over the washbasin; to the past, when they loved each other madly and unconditionally, and often found themselves stuck in police stations because of their frenzied passion; when life in Baku still flowed calmly and they began to live separately from their parents; when they no longer thought whether their poor-quality bed creaked or not, while the echo of their love filled the room...to the past, when little Zemma slept in a huge apartment in the Tbilisi courtyard, while Genna and Milla had sex everywhere: against the wall, on the floor, on the piano and, most often, on the massive wooden desk with its green rectangular cloth; to the past, when the world was tolerably painful, and the stench was not yet felt...

And when they return to reality, when Genna gets rid of all the memories that do not allow him to live, when Milla fully regains the time she has lost, and when they rewrite their unbearable past on each other's bodies, they will continue to live not only without noticing the hell around, but also forgetting all about its existence.

04:13

«*Ты чего не спишь?*»[59]
"And since when have you been sleeping with Mom?"
«*Не сплю, как видишь.*»[60]
"You made it up?"
«*Мы никогда и не сорились.*»[61]
"Then why didn't you talk to each other?"
«*Когда?*»[62]
"Well, I don't know. Almost always."

---

[59] Ты чего не спишь? (Russ.) -Why ain't you sleeping?

[60] Не сплю, как видишь (Russ.) I'm not sleeping, as you see.

[61] Мы никогда и не сорились (Russ.)- We've never quarreled.

[62] Когда? (Russ.) – When?

«*Бывает.*»[63]

"Happens all your life?"

"Life is very short to find the right words."

"Now stop being a toastmaster, will you?"

Genna smiles, goes to the kitchen, puts the kettle on the gas stove and takes the gingerbread out of the cupboard.

"Let's watch basketball, there is a good game on."

Lazare switches on TV. *Denver* vs *Oklahoma* is starting the second halftime and the *Nuggets* are one point ahead. One point in basketball is nothing, at least during the game, and in the end, it doesn't matter, at least for Genna, whether the winner wins by one point or twenty-one. He needs Oklahoma to win and Russell Westbrook to do a little miracle. Twenty-three points, twelve rebounds and six passes. Four passes more and Westbrook will get triple-double, repeat Oscar Robertson's record and become the second player in the history of basketball with a triple-double score in the season. Come on, Russell, come on! Somewhere in the Caucasus, in Georgia, in Tbilisi, in the region of the Tbilisi Sea, such a tragic person as Genna believes in you, and you have to get out of your way to justify his expectations and score not only a triple-double, but also a quadruple-double if needed! For Genna, tomorrow should be a different day!

The sound of a vibrating face massager from the "Formula of Youth" is coming from the bathroom—Milla is rejuvenating, removing the lost years from the pores of her face, dispelling millimeter after millimeter the heavy past from the numbness of her eyelids. Come on, Milla, come on! Erase everything bad and build a great wall, leaving not a single hole between the past and the present; and since you've decided to carry bricks, lay the foundation for the future too! Come on, Milla, come on! Tomorrow should be a different day!

Genna pours some tea for himself and Lazare, brings the cups into the sitting-room and sits comfortably in an armchair.

---

[63] Бывает (Russ.) – Well, it happens so.

"Here is your tea!"

"Thanks."

Genna knows his son too well not to know that sitting with such an expression on his face means that something bothers him, hurts him and doesn't give him rest.

«*Рассказывай.*»[64]

"What?"

"What's bothering you."

Lazare shakes his head, he doesn't want to talk...or rather, he wants to, but he can't. If he tells everything, he will have to confess everything, and if he confesses everything, then Lazare-Wu, created with such difficulty, will collapse and all his morality, Bushido and Hagakure will go to hell.

"Do you want it to eat you from the inside?"

It has already eaten him, and not only eaten, but also erased and threw away all the last tracks on which he worked..."Like the Messiah I'm living, crucifixion is my healing" he said, didn't he? And that crucifixion did not come without pain and without saying a word; one can't crucify oneself on a cross in secret and alone. Crucifixion needs a witness, so he says:

"Once you told me that it's easy to be a nonconformist when you're young."

"So what?"

"It turned out to be not so easy..."

And Lazare tells his Dad everything — he tells him about the class conflict, about the rich bastards and the poor who are on the verge of starvation; tells him about the debts taken from microfinance organizations; tells him what it is like to ride a moped in Tbilisi, breathing the air saturated with lead and exhaust gases; how it feels when you are hungry and others are full; what is *You order, We deliver*; he tells him about customers and delivery guys; about what it is like to leave your moped somewhere ten or even twenty times a day and each time be

---

[64] Рассказывай (Russ.) – Tell me.

nervous that it will be stolen, that you will lose your job, lose your miserable salary; that in this accursed life even those who work are lost, and the unemployed die so quietly and silently, as if they haven't lived at all, have never existed, never rejoiced, never wanted to eat, nothing hurt them; as if poverty is a fact that one needs to get used to and even got used to, because the elite, because to the elite, because for the elite...And Genna listens to him, and Genna understands everything he says, for his son is right, everything he says is true, but...Well, there are truths that don't justify one's choice, and Genna cannot justify his son for whose sake he could even claim that black was white; whom he never reproached; his son, for whose sake he himself would have stolen a moped...And despite the fact that Lazare sobs, suffers and repents, Genna still insists that a person is determined by his choice, and not by what he regrets; that his son made the wrong choice, which his father didn't expect him to make...He disappointed his father, but despite so many "*that's*," it is not too late. Now Lazare has two choices—either to correct his mistake, or live with it; and he says that Lazare...But Genna can't finish what he wanted to say, as he is interrupted by a terrible scream for help coming from the street. This scream is not a scream caused by the hardships of the 2000s; such screams turning into sobbing were heard in the nineties, several times a day at the windows of half of Georgia! The heart piercing scream repeats and Genna recognizes the voice of his friend Koba. He rushes to the window and sees that his friend is running limping, with a broken head, and several men in black masks, cursing and brandishing clubs are chasing him. They almost catch up with him, and if they catch him, they will inflict terrible injuries on him or even kill him! Genna looks at the windows of his frightened neighbors and sees the silhouettes of those hiding behind blinds; he sees how two men in masks drag Noogo out of the entrance door and squeeze him and Koba into the car; and he sees Zemma standing on the balcony with a pleased expression on her face, typing messages! He opens the window and begins to shout and swear and curse, and when he sees fear in his daughter's eyes, in her shaking hands and feels fear in her voice rattling with panic, his heart becomes so heavy that even Milla's vibrating massager cannot remove the heaviness from it. He rushes out of the apartment and down the stairs. Lazare and Milla with a cosmetic mask on her face, run after him. They are followed by Zemma, who screams desperately that it is her father and he shouldn't be touched, but the people in black masks have an order from above, and to fulfill that order, they are ready to sacrifice their own mothers, not to mention the father of some woman in a dressing gown. Thank God, the superior who has given them the order appears on time—he comes out from Noogo's entrance door and turns out to be Genna's childhood friend that has become a part of the system working in it under all governments. He is a former member of the *Mkhedrioni* paramilitary organization, a dark shadow from Genna's past and a witness to his sin; he is the person who read "Ivanhoe" to Genna and spoke about Umberto Eco; the man who lost faith in his own people and hope for a better future when, in parallel with the military coup in Tbilisi, a few kilometers from Rustaveli Avenue, a beauty contest *Miss Saburtalo* was held; who smelled the stench of the post-Soviet country much earlier than Genna did, but, unlike Genna, did not run away from it; on the contrary, he took it for granted and even adapted to it; from Noogo's entrance comes out the man whom Genna taught to ride a bicycle when they were still children; he comes out riding the very *Десна-два* with a *Тахион* saddle, which Genna considered missing for ages! The two childhood friends expected everything in the world except for this unexpected meeting. As they run into each other and turn to stone, the man from the ministry realizes that he can never be able to marry Zemma, while Genna feels how the ground under his feet begins to crack, erupting all the stench from the garbage chute...

and when Russell Westbrook makes a three-point shot and the commentator shouts: "What a perfect ending to a historic day," when the dramatic silence of the street frozen in the memories of the past was broken only by the sound of vibrating massager of the "Formula of Youth," Genna felt that not only his past and present, but also his future—his children grown up in the stench—were stinking.

ABOUT THE AUTHOR

Iva Pezuashvili is a contemporary Georgian writer and screenwriter. He is the current president of Pen Georgia. He graduated from the Feature Film Department of Shota Rustaveli Cinema and Theatre University. In 2011 he was the winner of the Autumn Legend, the student literature competition, with his story *Alchu (Lucky Toss)*. In 2012, he made a film *Babazi*, based on the story. He is the author of several TV documentary films and has worked on the script for the film series *Tiflis* since 2014. He has been publishing his stories in periodicals since 2012.

Intelekti published Iva Pezuashvili's debut book *I Tried* in 2014. His short story *Tsa* was one of ten short stories of Georgian writers published in 2018 by British publishing house Comma Press in the collection *The Book of Tbilisi* and one of seven short stories in the collection *Georgia: A Literary Invitation* published by German publishing house Klaus Wagenbach.

In 2018 Iva Pezuashvili was an honorable resident of the International Writing Program in University of Iowa and after that his first novel *The Gospel of the Abyss* was published by Intelekti Publishing. It was shortlisted for major Georgian literature awards. With his last novel, *Garbage Chute*, Iva won the 2022 European Union Prize for Literature as well as other literary awards, including the Tsinandali Award for best prose, and in 2021 he won the Special Jury Prize of the SABA award. His latest novel, *Mascarapone*, won the SABA Award for Best Novel of the Year in 2023.